THE TANGLING OF THE WEB

Sally, who married young to escape her appalling childhood, is often left to bitterly reflect on the hand she has been dealt. She is, on the whole, happy caring for her handsome husband, his mother, her own three children, one of whom has a disability, and her Walter Mitty sister. Then suddenly her world comes crashing down when her husband leaves her with no warning. With hard work and sheer determination she turns around a Leith pub which has a shocking reputation but still takes time to care for her ever increasing family. Finding answers to awkward questions which have troubled her all her life.

THE TANGLING OF THE WEB

THE TANGLING OF THE WEB

by

Millie Gray

Magna Large Print Books
Long Preston, North Yorkshire,
BD23 4ND, England.

British Library Cataloguing in Publication Data.

Gray, Millie
 The tangling of the web.

 A catalogue record of this book is
 available from the British Library

 ISBN   978-0-7505-3949-4

First published in Great Britain 2014
by Black & White Publishing Ltd.

LP

Cover illustration © Malgorzata Maj by arrangement with
Arcangel Images

Published in Large Print 2014 by arrangement with
Black & White Publishing

Magna Large Print is an imprint of Library Magna Books Ltd.

Printed and bound in Great Britain by
T.J. (International) Ltd., Cornwall, PL28 8RW

AUTHOR'S NOTE

This story tells of one family's life in Leith in the early twentieth century. Although it echoes some of the writer's experiences and personal feelings, the characters portrayed in the book are wholly fictitious and bear no relation to any persons, living or dead. Many of the street names, localities and other details from that period in Leith's history have been preserved, however.

In memory of my dear sister and friend, Rena McKinnon, who in her lifetime achieved the impossible.

ACKNOWLEDGEMENTS

Special thanks go to:

Celia Baird and my sister, Mary Gillon, for their continuing encouragement and support.

Gordon Booth, who set me on the path of novel-writing and continues to advise me.

Ian Grant for sharing his memories of being a young and raw police constable who pounded the Shore beat in Leith forty years ago.

The team at my publishers Black & White and in particular Karyn Millar for her meticulous editing and publicist Paul Eckersley for his ever-willing assistance.

1

1955

Her stiletto heels echoed shrilly on the stone stairway, causing her to realise that the noise may irritate her mother, and that was the last thing she wished to do. Bending down to remove the offending footwear, she breathed in deeply and exhaled slowly. Leaning on the wall for support, she reluctantly recalled that as a child she had often dreamt of and longed for this day. Relief seeped in when she also remembered that as she had matured the respectability that she was sure would come when she was able to say truthfully that her mother was dead had lost its importance.

In contrast, today the worry for Sally was just how she and Paddy Doyle, her mother's husband, were going to resist her mother's insistent pleas for them to put an end to her intolerable suffering. Sally sighed as she acknowledged that the agony of the pancreatic cancer had turned her formidable mother into a pitiful, grovelling wraith.

Tiptoeing towards the door of her mother's tenement home in Iona Street, Sally was convinced that she would always stand fast in her belief that to end someone's life, no matter

13

the circumstances, was murder. Nonetheless she knew Paddy Doyle would have no such qualms. Descended from a deported Irish criminal, he had been born and brought up in the Australian bush. This harsh upbringing had resulted in him being one of life's survivors who would crush anybody or anything that got in his way. Sally snorted as she was forced to grudgingly acknowledge that when he had married her mother he had also bestowed on her the respectability that she had long yearned for. But the price had been high – much too high, in Sally's opinion.

Forgetting that she was trying to make sure she did not disturb her mother with any undue noise, she sniffed loudly as she asked herself, *What kind of mother would treat her children the way Peggy had done? Her neglect and cruelty had been especially meted out to Josie, Peter and me.* Sally shrugged and sighed before going on. *Surely a cuckoo was more caring of her young?* Her thoughts were now fully consumed with memories of Peter, her beloved brother, and all he had endured. Always when she reminisced about the days of their childhood, anger bubbled up inside her and silent tears cascaded down.

PETER'S STORY
LEITH 1932

The sheriff looked from the slight, terrified, fair-haired fourteen-year-old Peter over to his mother. Whereas the boy was cowed, the mother was indomitable. He already knew from personal experience that she was a very handsome woman, but he had also perceived today that she lacked any maternal instincts or warmth towards her son.

Shuffling the papers in front of him, he sighed before saying, 'Peter Mack, you have been honest enough to confess to the stealing of two Scotch pies from the bakery in Dickson Street, and I accept that you did this because you were hungry so I am going to sentence you to be detained...'

Before the sheriff could continue, Peggy jumped to her feet. 'No, sir, I don't wish him jailed – give him several strokes of the birch!'

Around the court there were several loud intakes of breath. No feeling mother could wish her child to be treated in such a barbaric manner. It was true that up to the 1920s birching was regularly carried out in the police station in Leith, but a more enlightened view was now being taken on this practice and very seldom was any young person subjected to such cruelty unless the parents specifically requested it.

Sucking in his ample wobbling cheeks, the

15

justice hesitated. It was true that most parents who pleaded for the birch instead of a custodial sentence did so because they were living on or beneath the breadline. This meant that if the boy was earning, the loss of his wages would further impoverish the family. In Peter Mack's case his mother was a well-known accommodating Leith lady who plied her trade in Edinburgh. The lady was therefore supported by her many male admirers, which, he grudgingly admitted, included himself and several of his colleagues who served on the bench. This truth meant she would not starve even if her son was jailed.

Peter shifted nervously from one foot to the other as he waited for his fate to be announced. He was resigned to a good birching, where he would be stripped to the waist, tied by his hands and feet to a wooden bench and whipped by a six-foot-tall police officer with a five-sectioned birch whip. He gave an involuntary shudder when he realised this would mean that the skin on his back would be beaten black and blue and even torn from his bones. Shaking, he remembered that Jimmy Young, his pal, had told him to scream from the first lash. Peter knew he must do that because Jimmy had been lashed the year before and had decided not let out a whimper until he realised that his resistance to crying out only meant the constable would

16

lay it on heavier when he struck the next lash. Peter now swallowed loudly as terror engulfed him, and all he could do was to pray that the sheriff would be lenient and not say ten or even twenty lashes.

The clock ticked slowly by until the sheriff cleared his throat and said, 'Peter Mack, I accept that your mother left you and your sister for six days last week knowing full well that neither of you had any means of support.' He now stared directly at Peggy, who raised her finger and wagged it surreptitiously against her bosom to indicate that the judge, no matter how much he was prepared to pay, would never, ever enjoy her favours again. 'But a petty crime you have admitted to,' the sheriff continued, 'and as stealing cannot be tolerated, no matter the circumstances, I therefore sentence you...' He hesitated. All in the court could now see he was reluctant to finish his judgement. Nonetheless, after a few seconds he continued, '...to five lashes of the birch.' Peter gasped and buckled at the knees when he heard the leniency of the sentence and was further surprised to hear the judge wasn't quite finished with his deliberations. No, like Pontius Pilate he wished to wash his hands of the disgraceful judgement. So, staring directly at Peggy, he added, 'As requested by your loving mother!'

Immediately Peter was released into

Peggy's custody. But as was normal with her she wished not to be inconvenienced any further by this matter. So before going home she took him round to the police station for the punishment to be summarily carried out by the duty constable.

Peter never spoke to anyone, even Sally, about the thrashing he received at his mother's behest, but it was etched forever into his memory.

The tall, burly policeman who carried out the sentence did not appear to be a cruel man. In fact, when he tied Peter's wrists and ankles to the table contraption he asked in a concerned voice, 'Not too tight I hope, son?'

Peter, who was choking with terror, could only nod his head to indicate that the tethers weren't cutting into his skin. The officer then went ahead preparing Peter for the assault. However, before the beating began the policeman lifted the birch from another table and whacked the air with it three times. The whipping sounds petrified Peter and the constable asked again if he was feeling well enough for him to proceed. *What*, he wondered, *would be the point of saying, no, I'm shit scared, but Mister if I don't let you go ahead today then the beating I'll get from my mammy will be even worse than anything you do to me.*

Peter would always remember his screams as the birch tore at his flesh. The sounds were so high-pitched he couldn't believe they had been uttered by himself. Eventually relief overwhelmed him when the officer, with disgust, he thought, inflicted his last stroke. The constable then forcibly threw the birch as far away from himself as he could. The man then bent down and untied the inconsolable Peter's hands and feet, but before giving him some water to drink, the man gently sponged the blood from Peter's back. 'Your mammy didn't wait for you, son,' he then confided with a compassion that was beyond Peter's understanding. 'Said, she did, that you've to make your own way home to Ferrier Street.'

Peter staggered to his feet and inhaled deeply. He couldn't believe that breathing in could cause him so much agony. Picking up his shirt, he tried to put it on but could only drape it over his shoulders. Unsteadily, he then made his way out of the police station.

Once on the street, scalding tears cascaded down his face, but he made no attempt to wipe them away as every step he took was torturous, and he was sure that it was just a matter of time until he was on his knees.

After reeling and swaying his way over to Leith Links, he was glad when at last he was able to grip a rusty garden railing to support himself. Raising his head, he was pleased to see an unoccupied small bench nearby. Sinking onto the seat, he closed his eyes. 'Oh

19

Mammy,' he muttered to himself as the shock of what had happened engulfed him. Ferrier Street seemed miles away.

Four years later, Peggy further betrayed Peter and Sally when Paddy Doyle insisted she abandon her elder bastard children before he would marry her. She didn't even think twice before agreeing to the unnatural ultimatum.

When Sally and Peter arrived home from work that day they were shocked when they were told to gather up their belongings and leave. All that their mother added was that their eviction from their family home was with immediate effect. They tried to argue, but they knew it was useless. How could their welfare be important to their mother, Peggy Mack, when she wished, yet again, to share her bed with another man? This time her lover had said he would marry her but had laid down conditions. So all Peter and Sally could do was pack up and leave Iona Street, where they had recently been rehoused, without even being offered any sustenance.

Sally, who never forgot that Peter had been birched because he had stolen the pies to feed her, deeply regretted that they both were now homeless.

Staggering down the stairs with their worldly possession in some paper carrier bags, she felt an overwhelming desire to protect Peter. However, it seemed Peter felt he should be looking after her and she choked back her tears when he said, 'Never mind. And don't you get upset, Sally. I promise I'll find us something.'

That was what he thought would happen, but sixteen-year-old Sally knew she had a quicker solution to their plight. 'Peter,' she said, as she laid her two carrier bags at her feet, 'it's just a wee five-minute walk from here down to Halmyre Street. How about we go there?'

'Halmyre Street?' exclaimed Peter. 'Look, Sally, we have to stay realistic. How could we persuade the railway people that we are entitled to one of their hooses?'

'No. What I mean is until we get something else how about I ask Harry Stuart or his widowed mother if we could bunk in with them for a night or two? Then at the weekend we can look for digs.'

'But why would the Stuarts help us?'

Sally blushed before stammering, 'Because... Oh Peter, Harry fancies me and wants to marry me.'

'Marry you? But you're just a bairn – only sixteen. Oh God, you're no in the family way?'

'Of course not. I'm not like Mammy. I'm respectable. Probably take after my father.' Sally halted before drawling longingly, 'Whoever he was.'

Peter's bags were now lying beside Sally's

on the pavement. On looking up to the heavens for an answer, he was rewarded with a shower of hailstones that tore into his skin, reminding him of a birch cutting into his back. Sighing, he picked up the bags and uttered, 'Come on then. Let's see if Harry's mother has any Christian charity in her.'

Flora Stuart was one of those women who could be held up as the epitome of a mother. Like Sally, she wasn't much more than five feet in height; however, she did differ from slim Sally in that she resembled a warm, round dumpling. One of her other assets was her ever-smiling face, which beamed a welcome to Sally and Peter when she opened the door to them.

'Come away in then,' Flora chuckled as she stood aside to let them enter. 'And my, look at you – you're fair drookit,' she continued, picking up a towel from the back of a chair and offering it to Sally.

Murmuring a 'thank you', Sally firstly rubbed her hair and face with the towel before handing it to Peter. 'Mrs Stuart,' Sally continued, whilst wringing her hands together and indicating with a nod of her head, 'this here is my brother Peter and ... and ... and...'

'Sure, Sally, why are you so ... how can I put it ... oh aye, grovelling? Am I a monster or something that you're scared of?'

22

Sinking down onto a chair, Sally shook her head and wept. 'It's just... Oh Peter, can you say?'

Handing the towel back to Flora, Peter began, 'It's just that we need shelter for the night. I promise you that tomorrow I'll try and find us some digs.'

'Shelter? But your mother's house in Iona Street is bigger than mine here.'

Peter hung his head. His mother's promiscuity had always been a sore embarrassment to him and he just couldn't form the words that would explain why Sally and he were in such a predicament.

Sensing Peter's dilemma, Sally swallowed hard before saying, 'Our mammy's getting hitched to Paddy Doyle whom I wouldn't spit on if he was on fire,' she hissed before going on. 'And part of the marriage settlement – so it would seem...' Sally stopped to sniff in deeply and purse her lips, '...is that Peter and I are no longer welcome in our *family* home.'

Shaking her head from side to side, Flora looked about her home. Sure, she had three rooms and each had a bed in it. Flora herself slept in the bed recess in the living room; Harry, her only son, had the box room that was really just a large walk-in cupboard; and the other room was occupied by her nephew, Sweet William. 'Look,' she began, 'there's no a problem with me putting you up, Sally. After all, there's not much of you so you could bunk in with me.' She stopped to have a hearty chuckle. 'And would that not be suiting my Harry,' she continued, slapping her hands on her stomach, which sent a cloud of flour rising from her apron. 'But as to your brother here... Well, my Harry is a big boy, a very big boy, and with there not really being enough room for him in his single bed there is no way I could offer to let you share with him.'

Peter and Sally looked about the room and their eyes stopped when they looked past the open door and into the full-sized bedroom of the house.

Running her right hand over her hair before patting the chignon at the back of her head, Flora sighed before uttering, 'Sweet William, my sister's lad, sleeps in there. And okay, he has a double bed to himself, but Peter I couldn't let you sleep...' Flora gulped before hurriedly going on. 'Surely you know why he's called Sweet William?'

An uneasy silence fell in the room and was only broken when Flora said, 'Look. That's the bread fully raised again so I can get it in the oven.' Once the bread was safely in the oven cooking, Flora flopped down onto a chair. It then quickly became evident to Sally and Peter that she was thinking, and they were surprised when she jumped up and ran into the bedroom. 'But that's the answer,' she called back. 'William does nights at the train station, so Peter, if you could be up and out of the bed by half past six then it would work.'

'Just for tonight?' Peter tentatively asked.

'No. Until you get better accommodation than I can offer. Mind you, you will both have to pay digs and I will give William a wee reduction, a very wee reduction, to his dues.'

A satisfied smile came to Flora's face. Sally too was laughing because Flora would always help anyone in distress, but somehow her generosity had a habit of paying Flora well – very well. Was that not what Harry was continually saying about his mum: that always she was looking forward to a brighter future, which she was convinced her ingenious schemes would provide?

Without really speaking to anyone other than herself, Flora whispered, 'Saving up I am for one of those grand main-door houses in Easter Road.' She now stopped to do a jig around the table while adding, 'You know the rooms are that big you could hold a ceilidh in any one of them and not have to turn any of your generous kin folk away!'

The only consolation Sally had about Peter's life was her knowledge that the three years before he had gone off to war he had spent at Flora Stuart's house. Flora's was a home in the true sense of the word. A place

25

where Peter was always welcomed and well fed.

By the time Sally had stopped reminiscing, she had been standing at the door of her mother's house for ten minutes. She knew she had to enter, but she really wanted to flee. All she required to do was turn the key that was always in the lock and she would be in, but still that small action was beyond her. A small voice from deep inside her asked, *Are you going to stand here all night? What are you waiting for – some courage?* Before she could answer herself she became aware of someone approaching. Quickly Sally turned and found herself face to face with Luke, her stepbrother.

Today his silent stance was no different than what it always was – sneering and supercilious. 'Just catching my breath,' Sally murmured, thinking, *Why do I allow this upstart to unnerve me? So he thinks he knows who his father is. So what? Wonder what he'll do if he ever finds out that Mammy took Paddy, like all the rest of her conquests, for a hurl?* She shrugged. *But wouldn't that mean he could honestly say that he wasn't the offspring of a monster like Paddy Doyle?* Shaking her head from side to side, she silently agreed, *If that is the case then it would be best for me to keep mum.*

Once the door was opened, Luke and Sally advanced along the hallway. Sally had intended to go straight to her mother's bedroom, but with Luke following so closely at her back she proceeded past the closed door and into the living room. Immediately she was confronted by her sisters – hysterical Josie and distraught Daisy.

'Where have you been?' Josie demanded of Sally. 'I've been calling out for you.'

'Calm yourself, Josie. Are you saying Mum has passed...?'

'She will be any minute now,' Josie sniffled. 'Oh Sally,' she continued as she wiped her dripping nose with the back of her hand, 'Paddy threw us all out of the bedroom a minute ago and he said, "Enough is enough," and I don't think he meant us all weeping and wailing.'

Sally turned, pushed past Luke and raced in the direction of the bedroom.

Before throwing open the door, Sally breathed in deeply. Stepping into the room, she exhaled and balked at the smell of her mother's decaying flesh. Nonetheless, she had to lay aside her revulsion when the sight of Paddy bending over her mother with a pillow in his hand sent shock waves through her.

Although she was no physical match for Paddy, she immediately kicked off her shoes and slammed the door shut. Jumping up

27

onto the bed, she began to wrestle the pillow from him. 'What do you think you're doing?' she spat through gritted teeth.

'It's what she wants – an end to it all.'

Sally looked down at her emaciated mother and noted that she weakly nodded. Then, through laboured breathing, Peggy murmured, 'But first I wanted ... to say ... to you ... that I'm ... sorry.'

'Look, Mum, you don't require to apologise to me. It was all so long ago and I'm doing fine now.'

Peggy was now plucking at the bed covers and again she tried to speak, though this time it was only audible to Sally. 'Not you, Sally. You see, the pain has been so bad those last few days I wondered if anyone else in this world had ever suffered like me.' Peggy, her face now awash with tears, paused. 'And,' she began again, 'I got to thinking ... about my ... Peter.' Her breath was now coming in short pants and she paused before sobbing out, 'And it's him, my wee canny laddie, who I wronged, that I need ... for ... give ... ness ... from.' Peggy tried to grasp Sally's hand before pleading, 'Are you positive ... ly sure ... he was never...?'

She couldn't go on. She didn't need to. Sally knew exactly what was troubling her. Peter, Sally's beloved Peter, had only been twenty-one when war broke out and of course he was one of the first to volunteer.

Memories came crashing into Sally's mind. The emotional waving him off at the Waverley train station. His embarkation leaves before going to France and then El Alamein. The arrival of the impersonal telegram stating he was missing – presumed dead! Heartless Peggy, their mother, saying, 'Look, Sally, don't waste your tears. At least he has done the right thing and died. It would have been worse if he, like some others, had come back a cripple requiring looking after for the rest of his life.' Peggy's callous remarks had made Sally hysterical, but even her heart-rending sobs had had no effect on Peggy, who blundered on. 'And Sally, have you forgotten that it was thanks to Dunkirk that your precious brother survived another three years, which is more than most soldiers do?' Finally Sally recalled his precious letters. He never specifically asked about his mother. All he would write was, 'How is the grand duchess getting on?' Sally never mentioned their mother in her letters back to Peter. She didn't want to lie to him; nor did she wish to say that Peggy, as usual, was uninterested in his welfare. *Why*, she asked herself, *was it that me and all my siblings yearned to be loved and recognised by our mother – this woman who is now reduced, through pain, to the pathetic ugly creature who could only beg for compassion and an end to her agony. I wish*, thought Sally, *I had been able to snuff out all the suffering your indifference and cruelty caused.*

Six agonising minutes elapsed before Paddy and Sally came back into the living room. Sinking down on a chair, Sally mumbled through her tears, 'It's all over. She's gone.'

'You let him kill her!' Luke accused.

Shaking her head, Sally looked up and, staring directly into Paddy's eyes, she croaked, 'No. It was her time to go and she slipped away. Just gave up the ghost, she did.'

Paddy nodded and mouthed a discreet 'thank you' to Sally.

The gesture, however, was noted by Josie, Daisy and Luke, who looked at one another before Luke spat, 'And I hope you think the doctor who will be signing her death certificate will swallow that.' Without uttering another word, he raced from the room and into his mother's bedroom. Bitter sobs racked him as he gazed down on Peggy's now peaceful countenance. Picking up her hand, he kissed it gently before silently whispering, 'I know my dad did for you, Mum. I also know that he'll get away with it because that liar, your apparently upright and honest daughter Sally, is his witness.' His tears were now raining profusely down onto his mother's face as he falteringly added, 'I know, Mum, that I'm too young just now to get vengeance for you, but I promise you that one day I'll make him and that traitor Sally pay!'

Flora, seated at the table, was supposedly reading the newspaper, but in reality her thoughts were on her daughter-in-law, Sally, whose mother had finally passed away the day before. She gave a sly chuckle as she looked about the elegant living room in Elgin Terrace. She remembered vividly how her dream had been to save up enough from the rental of her croft in Culloden for a deposit on a ground-floor flat in Easter Road, but then Sally and her brother Peter had entered her life. Her dreams then became Sally's property, and when this Elgin Terrace main-door house with the added attraction of having some basement rooms had come on the market that was it. Nothing else was good enough now for Sally, and they could afford it if Flora pitched in the meagre rental she got from her Highland croft.

Giving an involuntary shudder because she now felt cold, Flora rose to put another shovel of coal on the fire and laughed out loud when she remembered that Sally had changed the fire from coal to a gas miser and all she was required to do was switch it on and soon the room would be as warm as toast. She wasn't, however, done with reminiscing. No, she now looked about and admitted that it was just great having so much living space. And Sweet William just loved having the basement flat all to himself

– especially now the family had grown since Sally and Harry had married in 1937. Without waiting, they went on to provide Flora with three grandchildren: Margo, who had reached fifteen and had just started work in the bank; little Helen, now nine going on ninety; and last but not least, poor wee eight-year-old Bobby.

Before her thoughts strayed to the biggest worry in her life – Bobby's short leg – the door opened and a bleary-eyed Sally entered.

'Did you manage to sleep, hen?' Flora enquired, rising to go into the kitchen to fill the kettle.

'Just on and off. Honestly, I just wonder how everything will work out now that Mammy's gone.'

'And why would you be concerning yourself about that? After all, when have any of them ever thought about us? And when you and I had to go out scrubbing when we first got this house, did any of them put their hand in their pockets and help us out?'

Sally nodded before saying, 'To be truthful, I don't give a monkey's uncle about Paddy or Luke.'

Flora made some clucking sounds and sniffed loudly, which was the usual sign that she was going to ask a question that was none of her business. 'And, eh,' she speered, 'talking of Paddy, did you manage to keep him from...?'

'There was no problem,' Sally interrupted before Flora could finish. 'In fact, he actually behaved himself.'

'Don't suppose you know about the funeral arrangements?' Flora, whom no one could convince that a wild animal like Paddy would ever behave appropriately, asked.

'No.' An uneasy silence fell between the two women until Sally asked, 'Do you think I should have all the children attend the funeral?'

'Take them to a graveside?'

'No. It will be in the crematorium at Seafield.'

Flora sniffed again. 'Suppose it is their granny.'

'Aye, but she was no better a granny than she was a mother.'

Silence descended again until Flora, who was always trying to make things easier for Sally, asked, 'I suppose your mammy wasn't made the way she was. I mean, nobody is born ... heartless.'

Sally gave a sarcastic chuckle. 'That's where you're wrong. Her parents couldn't take her indifference either and got rid of her as soon as they could.'

'That's what I mean,' Flora said defensively, 'your mammy herself wasnae treated right so she didnae know that bairns should be treasured and not...'

'Used as punch bags...'

Flora realised the subject should be changed, so, grabbing the teapot, she poured out another cup of tea for herself. 'Now,' she hesitantly began, 'if you're going to take our wee fellow to the service will you not be needing to go to that Polish shoe repairer up in Restalrig Road to see if he's managed to build up Bobby's shoe. You know how self-conscious he is about people seeing him limp.'

Looking up at the clock, Sally nodded. 'Look, first I'll finish my tea. Then I'll go and pick Bobby up at the school and take him to get his shoes.'

'Does he need to go? Could you not just pick them up?'

'No,' was the emphatic reply. 'Davidovich will want to see that he has done the alterations exactly to the specifications.'

The shrill, impatient ringing of the front doorbell caused Flora, who was dozing, to rise and run to answer the summons. Before she left the room, she smiled sweetly to Josie and Maggie, who were also startled by the pealing. She was only halfway along the hallway when she noticed through the half-glass panel that the bell-ringer was none other than her grandson, Bobby. Opening the door, she hissed, 'Why on earth are you ringing the bell? You know just to come in.' Looking beyond him, Flora could see

Bobby was accompanied by his mother. 'And you too, Sally, do you think I've nothing else to do but answer the door to people who stay here?'

Sally smiled. 'Look, Flora, just go back up the hall and pay attention to Bobby.'

Flora did as she was bid and then Bobby started to walk towards her. Walk towards her *without* a limp. And because Sally had got the headmaster to agree that he could wear long trousers to primary school, you couldn't even notice that one of his shoes was built up.

'So what do you think?' Sally crooned. 'Now do you still think I was throwing away good money on a craftsman doing the job?'

Shaking her head and not wanting to speak because she was choked with tears, Flora ran towards Bobby and embraced him. Looking towards Sally, she managed to mumble, 'You've got visitors.'

'Visitors?'

'Aye. Your pal Maggie and your sister Josie.'

'Maggie, well she'll be no bother, just sit her in the corner and she never says a dicky bird. But our Josie, now she could be ... bad news.'

Even although Sally was apprehensive when she bounced into the living room, nobody, especially Josie, could have suspected she was anything but happy to see her.

Josie decided she should take the initiative and before anyone else could speak she blurted out, 'Paddy, you know your pal and our erstwhile stepfather, has flung me out.' No one replied and Josie continued after a snort, 'And here's me left my job early so I could travel up here to look after Mum and the minute she dies I'm given the bum's rush.'

'But why? I would have thought he would have waited until after the funeral.'

'He would have done, but he found out that when I came up here I was on the re-bound.'

'Rebound?' Sally exclaimed. 'But I thought you were marrying that guy who is studying human behaviour at Cambridge, no less?'

Josie looked down at her feet, and although she was speaking to Sally it was her feet that got her attention. 'He did have the university's scarf right enough, but it turns out that his mother bought it in the hope someone would be fooled into thinking he was an under- or post- whatever graduate and give him...'

'The time of day?' interrupted Sally.

'I know you think I'm a fool. But you met him and you thought at last I had landed a good meal ticket.'

Sally grimaced and Flora started clearing the table.

'So, Sally, are you going to put me up?'

'Well, you would need to squeeze in with...' She was just about to say 'Flora', but Flora was indicating behind Josie's back that no way would she share her bed with Josie.

'Look, could you not just stay at Mum's until after the funeral and then you'll be able to think about your long-term future?'

Josie sighed before flashing her eyes to the ceiling. 'Oh Sally, you are so naive. Can't you understand that my life is so difficult because all men find me irresistible?'

Sally gawped. An answer was expected from her, but nothing that wasn't quite what Josie wanted to hear came into Sally's mind.

'And Paddy is flesh and blood,' Josie blundered on, unaware that no one was answering her, 'and even although Mum is not yet cold I have to accept he cannot trust himself to be alone with me.' She paused before whispering, 'And that and that alone is the real reason he asked me to leave!'

'Here we go again,' Flora, who had started lifting up the last of the dirty cups from the table, whispered to Sally, who did not respond.

Josie then went on to elaborate. 'Oh Sally,' she sighed, 'I know you and Flora being plain and homely don't understand that instead of my beautiful face being a blessing ... it's a curse. Every man who looks at me wants to possess me – control me – have me for his lover, and I'm only one woman. So how can

I satisfy so many?'

Sally stayed mute, because all she could think about was Josie and her problems with men, which had surfaced when she was much too young to have had such liaisons.

It also had to be acknowledged that since Josie had returned from Blackpool seven years ago, she had always gone away in the spring to work in hotels and in the winter she returned to stay as Sally's guest because their mother wouldn't have her or anyone else who wasn't prepared to pay their way.

The only reason that Josie had been staying at her mother's for the last two weeks was because Peggy was near death and required round-the-clock nursing care and she was so weak that she couldn't summon up the energy to throw Josie out.

JOSIE'S STORY
1936
Six-year-old Josie had just returned from school to find that her mother was yet again in the bedroom. By the huffs and grunts that echoed out of the room she knew better than to disturb her mother, who was obviously entertaining some man or other.

Since her mother had got older, and had become less in demand by the up-town gentry, her goal had been to get a man, any man, to marry her and provide for her. This aim should have been easy because Peggy, despite her advancing years and lifestyle, was still a beautiful woman, although she was now developing a widow's hump.

During the last two years, several men had come into her life but unfortunately also left it. But as soon as Paddy Doyle, a muscular young Australian, had arrived on the scene she was determined to snare him.

Josie looked about her and was pleased to see a tin of syrup and some bread lying on the table, so she began to spread a piece for herself. She had been so liberal with the syrup that it was oozing over the edges of the bread and onto her fingers. She had just laid her piece down and was starting to lick her fingers when Paddy Doyle emerged from the bedroom dressed only in his combination underwear. Slinking as unobtrusively as she could round to the far end of the table, Josie's eyes never left Paddy's face.

'Never seen a man in his drawers before?' cackled Paddy.

Josie, still licking her fingers, shook her head.

Paddy then squinted long and hard at her, causing a deep flush to rise from Josie's neck and up her face. 'Like your mammy you are.'

'I am?' stuttered Josie.

'Aye, a real beauty if ever there was one.' Paddy was now smiling broadly. 'Mind, you might have the face that will drive a man wild, but like your mother your arse will always be the right height for my boot.'

Josie didn't try to defend her short stature. Her reluctance to retaliate came firstly from knowing that being very small had its advantages – like people being exceptionally kind to her, as they thought her little more than a baby. However, now that her mother had come into the room, the consequences could be far-reaching if Peggy heard her speaking to Paddy.

'Paddy, don't you be filling her head with rubbish,' Peggy warned, with a meaningful glare at both Paddy and Josie. 'Good-looking she may be, but listen, and listen good, it will be a long, long time before she will be stepping into my shoes.'

Before Peggy realised what had happened, Paddy had advanced towards her and imprisoned her in his arms while rasping in her ear, 'Aye, lady, but remember I won't tolerate a wife who might get too big for her boots, and never ever, if you value your life that is, imply that I would tarnish pure innocence.' Without warning, he began to drag Peggy back into the bedroom. 'Whereas my lovely,' he muttered through gritted teeth, 'I don't mind how often I have to give a right good seeing-to to someone like you, who is as pure as the driven slush.'

Josie was just fourteen years old and about to leave school when George Grant told her she was the most beautiful woman he had seen in whole wide world. She was just so flattered she didn't take into consideration that thirteen-year-old George hadn't seen much of the world, as he had never ventured any further than the top of Easter Road. George then confided he was so in love with her that he would be treating her to the pictures with a coconut ice added in. 'You will?' exclaimed Josie, who just loved going to see all the films. That was where she could escape into her make-believe world where she was tall and willowy as well as beautiful. She also knew that if ever she did get to Hollywood in no time at all she would make a name for herself. 'But just a minute,' Josie added when reality returned, 'where will you get the money?'

'Easy-peasy,' replied George. 'See the fish shop down in the Kirkgate? Well, he also sells pigeons, and see me...' He now stuck his fingers through his braces as he swaggered in front of Josie. 'Haven't I just asked him if he would be interested in getting his hands on a dozen freshly killed birds, and he's up for it.'

'He is?' crooned Josie.

'Aye,' replied George, nudging Josie with his elbow, 'and he will pay enough for the two of us to get chummy in the cuddly seats.'

41

He paused to savour the moment before adding, 'And if you are really nice to me I'll throw in...'

'A wee box of Cadbury's Milk Tray?'

'Naw. A couple o' penny dainties because I cannae even afford the coconut ice I promised you.'

Of course, George was not too bright and didn't realise that the pigeons in the fish shop were wood pigeons – a delicacy when cooked – and the pigeons that roosted in the railway yard were feral or, as the fish-shop owner put it, 'Rats with wings.' Naturally George was disappointed about the unreasonable conditions the fish-shop owner had laid down about the birds he sold. However, he was not as piqued as Josie, who, instead of being treated to a night of romantic entertainment, found herself reduced to licking a penny toffee cup while George tried to put his hand up her jumper.

In the summer of 1944 Josie began working in Crawford's Biscuit Factory in Elbe Street. There her horizons widened, and before she had said a final goodbye to George, Steve, the store-man in the factory, whose job it was to keep her supplied with biscuit tins, had fallen madly in love with her. Steve was so besotted with her that he even carried the tins straight to her station. The only problem was that he was supposed to do that anyway and his dilly-dallying at her station meant the other women workers had to go and fetch their own tins.

Fed up with the situation, the older women quickly told Josie that Steve was married and was the father of seven children – and not all by his wife, because he was known to have an eye for young, gullible lassies – and if she didn't mind could she give him the bum's rush before he was the father of eight. After much deliberation, Josie resolved to do just that and then vowed that in future she would only encourage well-heeled older men.

Three months later, Josie was counting the days until she would be fifteen. It was about that time that news was being filtered out that now America had joined in the Second World War, Britain might emerge triumphant. This news excited Josie especially, as the bulletin said that they still required as many women who could be spared to join in the battle.

Josie decided there and then that what the country needed was her. So she marched into the recruiting office, where she was disappointed to find out that she was too young for the battle zones but that they could use her on the farms howking tatties.

Peggy made no comment on Josie's news that she would be leaving to go down to live and work on a farm in East Lothian. She was, however, put out because since she had had

Luke, who was now nine, and Daisy, now five, she had relied on Josie to watch over them when she was out gallivanting with Paddy. Paddy, unlike Peggy, did comment on Josie's leaving. She was surprised and tears bubbled up in her when he said, 'Now remember you are my little princess. I'm your daddy and I'll kill any man who doesn't do right by you.'

Two weeks later, Josie joined the team on a Tranent farm. Three of the lassies were young, though not as young as Josie, who had advised them she was seventeen but was small for her age. Her short stature, she confided to them, was because she had been born three months premature when her mother had been frightened by a bogeyman. Feeling sorry for her, the girls immediately welcomed her into their circle.

Time off for the girls was usually at the weekend. 'How would you like to go up to Edinburgh with us on Saturday?' enquired Senga, who had appointed herself leader of the pack.

Noting that Josie seemed wary, Hetty quickly added, 'We don't go drinking and whooping it up. Oh no, we go to the canteen at the east end of Princes Street.' Hetty stopped to ensure she had Josie's full attention before disclosing, 'That's where all the soldiers, airmen and navy boys, who are mostly on embarkation leave, go to for a sandwich, a cup of tea and a wee birl around the dance floor with any of us lassies that turn up.'

'Hetty's right there,' Julie butted in, before adding, 'and just think, Josie, ours might be the last lassies' faces they'll see before they ... are ... no more.'

On entering the canteen, Josie could see that the main room was packed with young men representing all the branches of the forces and nationalities engaged in the conflict.

'Good to see you,' the canteen manageress said to Hetty.

'Just love to come and help you, Mrs Duff,' Hetty replied, grabbing Josie by the arm. 'And this here is Josie, our new pal, and she wants to help too.'

Mrs Duff's smile radiated towards Josie. 'And what would you like to do, dear?'

Josie shifted uneasily. 'Wash dishes or I could sweep up.'

Mrs Duff, Hetty and Senga laughed in unison. 'No, my dear,' chuckled Mrs Duff. 'Someone as pretty as you we need to entertain the boys.' Josie was surprised when she then bent her head towards her to whisper, 'Now some of our lads are not able to read or write very well, so you could help there by reading or writing their letters for them.'

Eyes widening in alarm, Josie shook her head vigorously. Truth was, not only were some of the men not as literate as they should be, but neither was she. Noting her unease, Mrs Duff quickly asked, 'Could you take on changing the records on the gramophone then?'

Looking over towards Julie, who was jiving with an airman, Josie nodded enthusiastically before responding, 'Yes, and I can dance too!' Then, to Mrs Duff and Hetty's amusement, she sashayed across the floor in time to Glenn Miller's 'In the Mood'.

The winding up of the gramophone and the changing of the records, however, couldn't be done by Josie because she was just too busy dancing with her many admirers.

During a short interval, a fair-haired man sidled up to her. Josie was delighted to see him because, like herself, he was on the short side. Staring long and hard at him, she noted that he was at least half a foot taller than she was. Sniffing, she thought, *Aye, he's the right height for me, right enough, but measuring a mere five and a half feet he would be considered by most to be on the small side for a man.*

Roy Yorkston was obviously short in stature; however, he did not see this as a disadvantage and he pushed aside the other men who were anxious to attract Josie's attention. Then, with a disarming smile, he asked in an American drawl, 'Care to dance the night away with me, babe?'

How could she refuse? Her throat was dry. Her knees wobbled. *Surely*, she thought, *I am Cinderella and he is Prince Charming.* From that moment on, no matter who asked her to dance, she was only available to Roy. Staring into his deep blue eyes, she thought, *Oh, surely he and I were fated to meet.* Losing all sense of reason, she went on to suggest to herself that somehow the war had been deliberately contrived by the gods so they could meet!

Mrs Duff was a bit concerned. This wee lassie, she was sure, was not as old as she claimed to be – or even worse, she was completely naïve and unaware of the dangers of the real world. Risking being told to mind her own business, she meandered over to Josie, who was being pinned against the wall by Roy, who was sensuously licking her lips, nose and eyelids.

Hauling Roy away from Josie, Mrs Duff hissed, 'Look, son, I don't know how they do things back in your country, but here when a lassie needs her face washed she goes over to the sink and douses it with some clean water.'

'No need to rescue me, Mrs Duff. You see, I prefer him licking my face to him pushing his tongue down my throat,' Josie murmured whilst giving Roy a beaming smile.

'And there'll be no more of his putting his

47

tongue down your throat either,' gasped Mrs Duff, her cheeks now burning with embarrassment. 'This here is a Christian establishment where we're not into cannibalism.' Being in need of reassurance, she stopped to brush her hands over her ample bosom before adding in a voice racked with sobs, 'Supported by the Salvation Army we are.'

Roy put out his hand to touch Mrs Duff's arm, but she pulled back from him. 'Look,' he said, 'I know you think I've just met Josie and that I'm chancing my mitt. But believe me when I say that I know she is the girl I'm going to marry.'

'What?' shrieked Mrs Duff.

While Josie thought, *Oh, yes please.*

Pretending not to have heard Mrs Duff's exclamation, Roy continued, 'And right now I'm going to walk her home and speak to her parents so that they know my intentions towards their daughter are honourable.'

'Huh,' was Mrs Duff's first response before adding gleefully, 'And how long do you think it'll take you to walk to Tranent?' Roy shrugged, so she continued, 'Don't you realise that, unless you are a crow, it is at least a seventeen-mile trek!'

Instantly Roy's enthusiasm seemed to wane, until Josie said, 'But tomorrow's Sunday, my day off, so I won't be going back to Tranent tonight by bus or walking.' Linking her arm through Roy's, she looked up into

48

his eyes and simpered, 'I'll be going down to Elgin Terrace to stay with my sister Sally.'

Passion appeared to have been given the kiss of life and Roy bent down to brush her lips with his as he enquired, 'And where is Elgin Terrace?'

'Just a ten-minute walk away,' was Josie's jubilant reply as she steered him towards the exit.

In the initial three months of the courtship, the romance gained momentum. Josie was completely under Roy's spell. The power of his stories, which were always about what her life would be like in America when she arrived there after the war, were spellbinding. The bewitchment even had her forget the warning of her stepfather, Paddy, that she should always keep her hand on her ha'penny. She didn't of course know what he meant by that. It was like the warning that Flora Stuart always gave her in that she should not bring any disgrace down on Sally. She never said what the disgrace was, and if Josie asked her she would reply, 'Never you mind what it is. Just you don't bring it to this door.' The other problem with this warning was that whenever Flora had to talk about the facts of life she would sniff long and loud before picking up a duster and begin vigorously attacking the furniture. Facing the wall, she would then splutter, 'Don't you bother yourself about the facts of life. All you need to know is that every man from the age of thirteen dreams night and day about nothing else.' Treating Josie to a half-turn, she would quickly expand, 'And missy, now you have been brought up staunch Protestant since you came here last year, it is your solemn Christian duty to make sure their dreams never come true.'

These warnings she did try to adhere to, but as Roy was showering her with presents of fabulous nylons, chocolate and chewing gum, Josie had a dilemma. What beautiful and precious gift could she bestow on him? As per usual she was hard up, and in addition to that, war-ravaged Britain was putting all her productive efforts into creating ammunitions to annihilate the Germans and very little effort was going into the manufacture of quality gifts for the likes of Roy.

Slowly she realised that it was a losing battle for her to keep her virginity – or that was what she tried to convince herself once she had made up her mind. As both Roy and she were now so sexually frustrated, what would be wrong with surrendering the most precious of gifts? After all, Roy was her life's true love and there would never be another man in her life after him.

However, in her mind there still lingered the nagging warnings that she thought meant that you should never get so infatuated with any man that you would forget to keep yourself pure! *But do they?* she argued. These warnings, she concluded, were always couched in a language she didn't fully understand. Ambiguity was always there, so did she need to give them a second thought?

All her life she would remember Roy and herself climbing up Arthur's Seat as twilight shrouded them. It was one of those times in the middle of winter that was called a Buchan warm spell, when you were duped into believing spring had come early. Usually a three-day warm spell would arrive at the beginning of December, but here was another one in February. Holding Josie's hand firmly in his, Roy climbed up from the shore of the loch towards the ruin of St Anthony's Chapel. Once he was satisfied they were alone and hidden from view, he took off his overcoat and threw it down on the ground. It didn't seem to matter to them that night in February 1945 that the moon was casting fleeting, ghostly, ominous shadows around the broken walls of the chapel and over them. All that concerned and consumed them was their impatient and ardent love-making.

Six weeks later they were again up on the historic hill and they made love just as passionately as before but now with added tenderness. Afterwards, he gently stroked her

51

face and whispered, 'Oh, my little angel, you will have to be brave.'

She nodded. 'I know, but I didn't think you had guessed.'

Sitting up abruptly, he challenged, 'But how could you know? It's top secret that my platoon is being sent off to the front tomorrow.'

Without warning, Josie began thumping Roy on the chest. 'No. No,' she pleaded. 'I won't let you go. Oh Roy, you're needed here. We are to be married.'

'And we will be,' he reassured her, 'just as soon as I get back.'

'No! We need to marry before you go tomorrow,' Josie protested.

'Why? You know I will come back for you.'

'But what will I do if you take too long?'

Roy looked into her face and he could see the panic in her eyes. 'Are you saying...?'

She nodded as sobs racked her.

'But it's only six weeks since we started ... well, you know, what we've...'

'Maybe so,' shrieked Josie. 'But I know I'm away with the goalie because I've ... missed. Three weeks late I am and spewing up every morning.'

'Oh God, what am I going to do? If I don't turn up tomorrow I could be shot for desertion.'

'And if you don't do right by me you'll be kicked to death by my stepfather, Paddy.'

'Look, little one, the war in Europe is nearly over. There's just mopping up to be done now. So I'll be back in a few weeks' time.' Josie rocked from side to side and he drew her in close to murmur, 'You must be patient and wait till then.'

Trembling all over, Josie mumbled, 'You should also know I've just turned fifteen!'

'What does that mean?'

'That I'm a minor and I could have you arrested for doing what you did to me. And I will be believed when I tell them how much it hurt.'

Roy gulped. 'But it was your idea. And tonight you said it was lovely.'

'Yes. Now it's lovely.' Josie began crying profusely. 'But at first it hurt so badly – I bled real blood.'

Roy got to his feet and starting pacing about while Josie continued, 'Look, love, why don't you just forget about the army and stay with me. Then next year,' she babbled on as she clasped him around the knees, 'when I'll be sixteen we can get married.'

Struggling to be free of Josie's hold, Roy spluttered, 'Just a minute. First of all you demand that I marry you straight away. Then you tell me you're not old enough to take your vows.' Sheer desperation caused him to wave his hands in the air. 'You were even too young to have led me on the way you did.'

Josie sank to the ground again and began to sob, this time uncontrollably. Roy, not knowing what to do, knelt down beside her. He acknowledged that he did love her and in reality she was just a child who needed his protection. Drawing her into his arms, he murmured, 'There there, my darling. I'll stand by you and put everything right, but... I have to report for duty in the morning.'

He stayed with her until the sun came up. The beautiful sun that signalled it was time for him to report for duty.

Roy had just left for his combat calling when Josie decided that before he could return to her the mess she was in would soon be evident for all to see.

So who could she turn to? No use approaching her mother, who never had been really interested in her or what she was doing. As for Paddy, he would be so disappointed that he would just wash his hands of her. Josie sighed before acknowledging the only person who'd ever shown her any kindness and understanding was Sally. She could turn to her. However, there was just no way Sally would be able to solve this problem for her. Josie reluctantly accepted that the only person who could help her was herself. Which meant all she could do now was to run away. Put miles between herself and her family. If she didn't, not only would she be the laughing stock of the whole community, but people would also say she was like her mother – a slut!

Even if her life had depended on it, Josie could not remember why she decided to go or how she got herself to Morecambe. It was true that Josie was not very bright, but what she did have was animal cunning, the most valuable of all the instincts, and this attribute meant she had the desire to survive at all costs.

The first thing she did on arrival at the resort was to go direct to a vicarage and confess her sins to an Episcopalian cleric. He appeared to be sympathetic and non-judgemental, but then Josie had said she had been raped by a man she didn't know. This explanation made the vicar realise he must put her in touch with a home for unmarried mothers.

Mrs Coggins, the lady in charge of the home, grimaced when Josie refused to give any details of her family. 'Don't you realise, my dear,' she simpered, 'that this unholy war has resulted in not just tens but hundreds of young people like you asking for our help?'

Josie did not respond.

'So if it is at all possible,' Mrs Coggins continued, 'we require to be given the information that is necessary so that we can liaise with your family. Believe me, that is the best way to deal with this situation.' Mrs Coggins paused to point a finger at Josie's stomach. Josie still did not speak, even though Mrs Coggins was now drumming her fingers furiously on the table. 'Look. We do require information about your background, so please...'

The plea, however, only resulted in Josie shrugging her shoulders again. After a long, uncomfortable pause, Mrs Coggins lifted a handbell from her desk and rang it vigorously. The summons was answered by a young pregnant woman, who was then instructed by Mrs Coggins to take Josie to dormitory five and to allocate her a bed.

The months she had to endure in the hostel without the support of Sally or any of her friends from home dragged for Josie. Every day for the first three months she would go out for a walk and post a letter to Roy. Never in the letters did she say anything other than how she was and where she was staying. She had hoped he would come and rescue her, but by the fifth month of her pregnancy she concluded he had abandoned her. For the next month, every night she cried herself to sleep, vowing she would get vengeance for herself by treating every other man that came into her life with the contempt he deserved.

November's chill winds were blowing when Josie's labour started. Their howling reminded her of their presence in February when she had willingly allowed Roy to get her into the mess she was in. Six hours later, the winds had ebbed to a breeze and Josie's agony came to an end. 'A beautiful little girl you have,' the midwife crooned. 'Look.' Now the nurse brought the swaddled child close to Josie's face. She found it difficult not to look. And it was true she longed to take the child in her arms, but she knew if she did that she would be unable to stick to her resolve.

To the midwife's astonishment, Josie turned her head away. 'Look. I have said, more than once, she must be adopted, so just take her now.'

'But surely you would like one little...?' protested the nurse.

Josie felt her determination waning, so to bolster herself she screamed, 'Just take her away!'

Two weeks later Josie left the hostel, but she didn't return to Edinburgh. For the next three years she worked in English hotels as a live-in chambermaid. During all of that time she had wanted to contact Sally and go home. She was always deterred by fact she would have to explain to the family why she had run away: to tell them the truth, which she certainly wasn't prepared to do.

1948
Josie was working as a chambermaid in a

hotel in Manchester. Her partnering work-mate, Emma, had a habit of annoying her by always spouting rubbish that Josie didn't wish to hear. To cope with this annoyance, Josie would just turn herself off. That was until the day she heard Emma utter, 'And the hotels up in Blackpool, now they have the illuminations up and running again, are crying out for staff. Wages are better than here; only drawback is it's seasonal. But see they Scots people, you know them that talk like you, they don't half tip well.'

'Scots folk?' queried Josie. 'But what have they to do with Blackpool?'

'Go for the September weekend so they do. Come down from Glasgow, Dundee and Edinburgh by the bus loads just to see the lights.' Emma paused and put a clean pillow-slip on a pillow, and as she pulled it straight she licked her lips and muttered, 'So it's so long to here and hello Blackpool for me.'

'When are you going?'

'Put my week's notice in yesterday.'

Before Emma could go on, Josie sped from the room and up to the manager's office.

Blackpool seemed to Josie to be just magical. Not only were the illuminations just fan-tastic but so were the fairgrounds, the theatre shows and of course the gypsy who told you your fortune once you had crossed her hand with silver – which had to be no less than two half-crowns.

Both she and Emma were employed in the same hotel. Not any hotel would have done: Josie she insisted that she would only work where people from Edinburgh had booked in for the autumn weekend. True, it was just July, but she was sure her plan would work. And didn't she now have the word of the gypsy who had read her hand. Oh yes, Gypsy Rose Lee had assured her everything would work out as she had planned. The only problem she could see for Josie was that of a man, not British, who had a grudge against her and would make trouble for her in the future if she riled him further. So she was cautioned to be careful.

When the buses arrived from Edinburgh in September, Josie was poorly with a cold. The hotel manager suggested that she should take some time off to nurse her affliction but she refused. As soon as the guests disembarked, she was down on the pavement asking if she could assist anyone with their cases.

She couldn't believe her luck when Flora Stuart replied, 'That would–' However, Flora, her mouth agape, broke off abruptly. 'Oh dear God in heaven please tell me I'm no dreaming,' she exclaimed. 'It is you, Josie, isn't it?' she hollered, holding Josie by the shoulders. 'But of course it's you. Nobody else could have such a bonny, bonny face.'

Josie wriggled herself free. 'Oh Flora, please don't tell anyone you found me,' she lied.

'That'll be right.' She stopped to ponder before adding, 'No, I won't tell them, because when I leave on Monday morning you'll be on the bus with me.'

During the whole journey from Blackpool back to Elgin Terrace, Josie rehearsed again and again what she was going to say about her disappearance. The only way she could justify her vanishing without telling anyone was to lie. This would pose no problem to Josie because it was an art she was now an expert at. To be truthful, she had told so many lies that she herself wasn't quite sure what the truth was about anything now.

So when Sally asked for an explanation, Josie was ready with her pat answer. Hanging her head, she began, 'Oh Sally, I have missed you so. B-b-b-but you have to try and understand why I couldn't tell you...' She paused to ensure she was having the right effect on her sister and, satisfying herself that she was, she drew in two deep breaths before hesitantly continuing through gushing tears, 'A man, who I thought was our friend, our friend, Sally ... tried it on with me and when I refused to be sullied by him he threatened to tell you all I had led him on!' She stopped again to wipe the tears from her eyes, then sighing loudly she slowly continued, 'You see

... he said that if ever I should tell anyone ... about his advances he would give me ... such a doing that nobody...' she stopped to run her hand over her face, '...would ever think me beautiful again!'

'And I bet I know who you're talking about. None other than that despot Paddy,' Sally hissed.

The words had just left Sally's mouth when Josie was gripped by terror. She had never meant to identify anyone, least of all Paddy, so quickly. Without a sign of a tear or a sigh, she added, 'No. No, it wasn't him.'

No matter how much she tried to convince Sally that in no way was Paddy to blame for her disappearance, Sally just wouldn't budge from her interpretation of Josie's story because that was what she wanted to believe.

Frustrated by Sally's reluctance to give her an answer as to whether she could move in or not, Josie suddenly lifted her suitcase up and banged it down on the table.

Sally, however, was completely oblivious to Josie's action. She was too busy thinking that there had never been any problem in the past with Josie moving in because Sally would have bedded her down with her two daughters. But Margo was now fifteen and working and was quite happy to share her bed with her nine-year-old sister Helen but would not be willing to do so with Josie, who reeked of cigarette smoke. But what really made things awkward now was that eight-year-old Bobby had problems with his legs and Sally always insisted he had a bed to himself.

Suddenly Josie broke into Sally's thoughts when she thrust a carrier bag into Sally's hand. 'What's this?' she asked, peering into the bag.

'Things of Mammy's. Dear Paddy,' she spat through gritted teeth, 'thought now that Mum was gone they really belonged to us. Tossed them out the door after me when he threw me out for no *good reason* other than...' Josie allowed her voice to trail off and she had the grace to blush slightly when she acknowledged she was not telling Sally the truth. No way could she bring herself to say, *Look Sally, he evicted me because he said he only put up with me squatting at Iona Street because Mammy was dying But now she is gone he wished me to know that he knew all about the slur I had put on his reputation. He even added that he knew the truth about me and if I wasn't careful to stay out of his sight he would tell everyone that I was nothing other than a lying, conniving slut.*

'Oh look, Josie, here in the bag is a bundle of letters addressed to you.' Sally flicked through the bundle to make sure they were all for Josie and halfway through she gasped. 'And most are from America.'

Wrenching the bundle from Sally's hand, Josie sat down and opened the first letter. 'Dear Josie,' it read, 'I know that, like me, your heart will be broken today. How cruel it was that my lovely son was killed in an automobile accident on the day he landed in France.'

Josie, her breath coming in short pants, rose up and, clutching the letters close to her bosom, ran from the room and into the bathroom. Sally immediately followed her but found that the bathroom door was firmly shut and locked. 'What's wrong, Josie?' she pleaded, banging on the door. 'Let me in. You know you can tell me anything.' But the door stayed firmly closed.

Sitting on the lavatory seat, Josie first put the letters from Roy's mother into date order and only then did she begin to read them. The first letter had shaken her and she wished she had confided her pregnancy to Sally. Had she done that she knew she would not be in the position today where she regretted her hasty and unnatural behaviour. The second letter only added to her distress in that Roy's mother had written that only now, some four months on, had she received her son's belongings and in it were Josie letters. She wished Josie to know that she was thrilled to learn her son would live on through a grandchild. Mrs Yorkston wrote that she would be delighted if Josie would travel to America, where she would be cherished and looked after, as would the child when he or she arrived. The third letter was pointedly critical of Josie's actions. Mrs Yorkston wrote that she had been in touch with the home in Morecambe and that Mrs Coggins, the matron, had advised her that Josie had given birth to her granddaughter. And for some reason that was beyond her comprehension, Josie had chosen not to keep the child and had handed her over for adoption, which was to take place very soon. 'Why could you not have trusted me?' the letter chided. 'All I want is to be able to love my son's child and be part of her life.'

Josie was now consumed with regrets and guilt. *Trusted you, Mrs Yorkston? I was fifteen, terrified and alone. You say that you wish you could have been part of Roy's child's life. Do you think I don't? Don't you realise that never does a day go by that I don't think of her? Worry about her? Wonder if she's having a happy childhood? Pray that it's not like mine was? No love. No laughter. All I ever knew were tears and abuse.*

Sally's insistent banging on the door again and demanding to be let in brought an end to Josie berating herself. Reluctantly, she rose up and unlocked the door.

'Look, Josie,' Sally began as she dragged Josie into an embrace. 'I've just been talking to Flora and she says it's natural you're upset, very upset, about Mammy dying. I didn't realise that, even for us, that it would be such a sad day when you lost your mother. Okay, she wasn't the best, but she was all we had.'

Josie began sobbing again. *Mother*, she thought. *That bitch that we call mother got my precious letters ten years ago. She opened them. Read them. Could have given me peace and joy and yet she let me suffer. Prolonged my agony, she did. Why? Dear God, please tell me why?*

By sheer force Sally had dragged Josie into the living room, and sitting her down on a chair and massaging her hands, she confided, 'Look, Flora and I didn't say, but Sweet William is leaving in a fortnight. His dad has died and he's going back to Smithton to run the croft for his mother.' What Flora and Sally had never told Josie was that William's father had turned him out of Smithton when he discovered that William was homosexual, but now he was gone William could go back to where his heart had ever been.

'But what has William leaving to do with me?' speered Josie.

'Just that Flora and I think that you should take over the wee basement flat when he vacates it. But no running backwards and forwards and leaving me with no rent while you do another season. You're twenty-five now. It's time to put down roots. You need to get a permanent job and make a life for yourself.'

Josie nodded.

'Just one thing more.' Sally hummed and hawed before adding, 'And no men staying the night. This is a respectable home. Oh, look at the time, Harry will be home soon and he's out singing tonight.'

HARRY'S STORY
1924

When Harry was just a wee lad of seven, he couldn't believe that at last it was holiday time from Lorne Street primary school.

This meant that sharp at six o'clock tomorrow morning he and his mother would be travelling on the train from Edinburgh to Inverness and then on to Smithton, Culloden. The journey to Smithton would be by pony and trap, an extravagance according to his mother, but as Granny had ordered the coachman to pick them up she had to thole it. Once they arrived at Granny's croft house, he knew his mother would moan about having to pay for the last leg of their journey. 'Mother,' she would exclaim, 'we have travelled all the way from Edinburgh to Inverness and not a penny has it cost us...'

'Aye,' Granny would butt in, 'because with your Colin working on the railway you get free passes for the trains, which are paid for by fare-paying customers like me.'

Flora wouldn't respond to her mother's

gripe except to say, 'And with what that highwayman charged me I wish to goodness the train lines extended to here.'

The other bonus with not having to pay for the train was when they boarded at Edinburgh, Harry's mother, wishing to appear prosperous, would proceed to the dining car and order breakfast. This was the place those who were considered to be doing 'better' dined. The tables were adorned with white starched table linen and brightly polished silver knives and forks. The menu was good and varied, but all Mum ever ordered for both of them was *one* plate of bacon and eggs with plenty of bread and tea.

Often Harry vividly recalled that when the train stopped at all the stations with the grand-sounding names, like Pitlochry, Kingussie, Aviemore and Daviot, with its quaint little church, he would count the number of people who got off the train and how many got on. He also liked to see everyone who would be boarding with hens, chickens and ducks in cages.

Harry loved going to visit his granny. Her croft house front windows looked down over the Black Isle, and a short five-minute walk through the woods at the back of the house meant Harry could be standing on the Culloden battlefield. It wasn't the tourist attraction then that it would become later, so in solitude he could play among the tombstones that marked the graves of the brave clansmen – his ancestors who were slaughtered there. Often he wondered about the stones that marked the graves of 'mixed clans'. Was it that they were from different clans or was it that parts of mutilated bodies were buried there? After pondering this, he would go and run and whoop over the place marking the fallen English.

There were so very many other things about Granny's that Harry loved, like her home-made bread, scones and pancakes, and his favourite, a large, warm, steaming clootie dumpling that she always made for him coming. For the three days it lasted, and he didn't mind if the delicacy was served hot, cold or fried.

Of course, Granddad always had chores for Harry to do and he looked forward to being kept busy on the croft, seeing to the hens, ducks, sheep and cattle.

The only thing that Harry didn't like about Smithton was he had to visit his aunt and her husband, whose croft house adjoined Granny's. This peculiar set-up came about because Granny had been left the holding by her father, who had gone to his grave lamenting that he had never been blessed with a son.

Granny had had the large house and land divided in two, knowing both that her days were numbered and that Aunt Shonag would need to support her husband. Shonag got her part immediately, and when Granny died the remaining half would go to Harry's mother, Flora, who, Shonag's husband said, should get no part of the land or house as she had made a life for herself in Edinburgh.

Aunty Shonag was so different from her sister, Flora, in that she gave the impression that, like her husband, she was very holy. She also dressed the way he thought respectable women should. This meant her continually donning, even in summer, a hat that Harry was sure was an old, badly hand-knitted tea cosy. The balaclava-type helmet was rammed so fiercely down on her head that not only were her brows and ears never seen but neither was her chin. To add to her submissive and unattractive appearance, she was always kitted out in a long black skirt, which brushed her stout shoes and thick, hand-knitted stockings.

Given pride of place in Fergus and Shonag's home was a painting that terrified young Harry. The likeness was of one of Fergus's malevolent great-grandmother. So high in esteem did Fergus hold his ancient Bible-bashing foremother that he had turned Shonag into her living image. Always when she was faced with Harry, she would chant, 'Children should be seen and not heard. Not heard.'

Harry would sigh and think, 'And who

would want to speak in this horrible, off-putting place anyway?'

From a very early age Harry was able to assess situations and detect where there was disharmony in relationships. He therefore realised that Fergus was a man who allowed no one an opinion that was different from his. His wife, who through her inheritance provided everything, obeyed his every command. She even chased after their cockerel on a Saturday night and made sure he was locked up in a shed by himself until Monday morning. This was done because her husband declared that he wished no ugly, wanton hens to be enticing his handsome rooster to dishonour himself on the Sabbath.

William, the only son of the family, was a different kettle of fish from his parents. Whereas his father was a strict disciplinarian, somehow William, who was five years older than Harry, viewed the world differently and always went about his day whistling.

As the years went by, Harry fell more and more in love with Smithton. He felt made welcome there by all except his aunt and uncle. Nonetheless it would always be a memory of great sadness for Harry that after blowing out the candles on his birthday cake, eighteen-year-old William blew away forever the pretence that his family was happy and united.

Harry always shook his head when he remembered how with a devilish smile and a cock of his head William stood at the top of the table and declared to the assembled family that he didn't wish to go a-courting Kristy McLeod, who had been specially invited to the celebration.

Rising to challenge his son, Fergus demanded, 'And why not?'

William smiled broadly to Kristy, who was blushing deeply. 'Look,' he began, 'try and understand that I've nothing against Kristy. In fact, if I was going to be interested in any girl it would be her.'

'What exactly are you saying?' Fergus bellowed.

'Just that...' William hesitated before adding, '...I'm simply not interested in girls.'

'Not interested in girls. Then who in the name of the good Lord are you interested in?'

'Donald – you know, the blacksmith down at Culloden House!'

A deep, ominous silence filled the room, which was only broken when Fergus banged his fist repeatedly into the middle of the celebration cake. The assembly just sat mute as the cake showered down and round about them.

Suddenly Fergus, eyes bulging out of his head, roared directly into William's face, 'An abomination in the sight of God: that is what you are!'

William stepped back and gave a non-chalant shrug, which further infuriated his father.

Dumbfounded by his son's attitude, Fergus now turned to face Shonag. 'And you, woman,' he screeched, causing her to flinch, 'do you *now* see what allowing him to take Highland Dance lessons has resulted in?'

Shonag tried to respond but was silenced by a flick of her husband's hand. 'Now to-morrow,' he spat with such ferocity his saliva sprayed onto his wife's face, 'by the first train to leave from Inverness, *you* make sure that that...' he paused to turn and point to William, '...freak you spawned is on it. And he is never, ever to return to *my* home again as long as I live. Do you understand?'

No matter what she thought, Shonag would normally just agree to what her husband wished. Not today. Grabbing the neck of her balaclava, she whipped the hat from her head. Harry gasped when the most beautiful, wavy blonde-ginger hair he had ever seen on a woman cascaded down. Running her hand through her now free locks, Shonag whimpered, 'No matter what he is or isn't – he is my son and he has been the only warmth and joy I have ever had in my life.' She paused, gulped in some air, looked her husband straight in the eye and further spat, 'Now, my dear husband, listen and

72

listen good, because if he goes ... then so do I!'

Granny jumped up and grabbed Shonag by the arm. 'How often have I told you that it was you who made your bed so you have to lie in it? Ogre he may be, but he is your chosen ogre, and because divorce is something no one in this family will ever sink to you'll just have to stay put.' What Granny didn't add was that there was no way she would allow the croft she had bequeathed to Shonag to be solely occupied by detestable Fergus, her wily son-in-law who had persuaded her weak daughter to put it solely in *his* name.

Harry remembered being taken aback that his gentle and fun-loving granny, as he had always seen her, was in fact the matriarch who ruled her family with an iron fist in a velvet glove. He was further surprised when Granny turned to his mother and stated, 'Flora, you and Harry will also be on the first train tomorrow and you will take William with you and give him a home in Edinburgh.'

'But...' Flora began to protest, but she was silenced when Granny took charge again.

'In the port side of Edinburgh where you have put yourself now, William will be quite at home.'

'He will?' screeched Flora.

'Sure. Do you know only last week Rena the milk was telling me that when she was down in Leith visiting her sister last month she lost count of the number of folk who didn't know which way to turn. So that means our William will not be out of place there.'

Fergus's coarse laughter echoed around the room. 'And her man,' he bellowed, pointing to Flora, 'if he is a man at all will not give houseroom,' he now signalled with a backward jerk of his thumb to William, 'to that poof!'

Shonag, who Harry thought had turned into a magical, beautiful person, looked pleadingly at Flora. Nodding her head, Flora went over to Shonag and whilst lovingly stroking her hair she whispered, 'My man is a good man. For sure I know my Colin will take your laddie in and not only welcome him into our home but he will also treat him as if he was our own son.'

Harry and his mother did return to beloved, beautiful Smithton but only twice after the family row. Their last visit was for the funeral of Granny. After the service, Flora approached Fergus and begged him to relent and allow Shonag to see her son, but he remained adamant. Unable to hide her contempt for him, she abruptly turned away, but she did vow to herself there and then that she would never, ever set foot in Smithton again as long as he breathed. The croft she had inherited was now to be rented out.

Harry never regretted William coming to stay in his home and, up to a point, Colin, his father, didn't either. It was just that when Flora truthfully told Colin why Fergus had banned his son from Smithton that Colin seemed to ponder before saying, 'The lad is welcome, but I don't think our Harry and he should share a bed.' This statement seemed to irk Flora, so to soften its effect Colin drawled, 'And tomorrow, if we all agree, that is...' He paused and looked Flora straight in the eye before continuing, '...I'll take him with me and get him a start on the railway.'

At first this decision about the sleeping arrangements annoyed Harry because William, being older and now a working man, was given his spacious bedroom and he found himself crammed into the box room.

Harry was never sure whatever way it happened, but as the years passed by he forgot about being inconvenienced by William and the two of them bonded as close as brothers. Harry would always be so grateful to William for the help and support he gave to his mother and himself when Colin had a fatal fall at work.

Up to that time, seventeen-year-old Harry, who had stretched to five feet nine inches and was fortunate enough to have his slim, athletic form complemented by light-brown wavy hair, twinkling blue eyes and an infectious smile, had never envisaged that his parents were mortal.

When his father was killed, it seemed to Harry that it was an unnecessary cruel blow and he found himself questioning God's wisdom. Why, he wondered, did the Almighty take such a good man as his dad before he had enjoyed the full biblical threescore and ten years?

Thinking that only weak men wept, Harry had sought out times and places where he could weep in solitude. One of these places was in William's bedroom, until William surprised him by coming home early. Harry was surprised then when William, instead of berating him, said, as he offered Harry a handkerchief, 'Here son, cry your heart out. If Colin had been my dad, I would be suicidal at his loss.'

To everyone's surprise, Shonag came down for the funeral. She had just got in the door when Flora said, 'Don't you be telling me you brought Fergus with you. I won't be responsible for anything I say to him today.'

Going over and firstly embracing her son, she replied, 'No. He is where he belongs – on his own.'

Cradling his mother closer to him, William, in a voice choked with sobs, managed to croak, 'But Mum, how did you mange to persuade him to let you come?'

Releasing herself from her son, Shonag

went over to sit on the arm of her sister's chair, where she gave a triumphant laugh. 'Well, as you all know, he is a man of strict religious beliefs and principles, so he never allows alcohol in his mouth. So when he forbade me to come down to pay my respects to a man I am indebted to, I just asked him to accompany me out into the cow byre, and going over to the back wall I removed one of the stones and lifted out the half-bottle of Johnnie Walker whisky that he keeps secreted there.' Everyone in the room was dumbfounded. Shonag then continued with a wicked little laugh, 'And handing Satan's brew to him I said, "Here, throw it right down and over your throat like you usually do. That way you can continue to say honestly that alcohol never touches your mouth!" I then threatened to tell the minister his secret and suddenly he was adamant that coming down here was the right thing for me to do. He was so pleased to let me catch the early train he even accompanied me to Inverness.'

Harry was still grieving the loss of his father when he went into the bakers at the end of Halmyre Street to buy a Scotch pie. The young lassie behind the counter smiled warmly to him before saying, 'Sorry about your dad. Nice man he was.'

Nodding, Harry felt his eyes well with tears, which spilled over when she added,

'No need to pay for the pie. Eat it right away because it's warm and it might ... well, it just might help.'

Immediately Harry started to devour the warm delicacy, and when he had finished eating he lingered on in the shop so he could get a better look at Sally. He liked the way she had tied her light-brown hair, her best feature, up in a red ribbon that matched her rosy cheeks. Although she was not as beautiful as some other lassies he had fancied, he did like the fact that she was always smiling and that the smile seemed to reach her twinkling crystal-blue eyes. All in all, she had a captivating inner loveliness.

Every day after that Harry called in for a pie, and every day the lassie smiled at him. After the first day he asked her what she was called, and after a week he got up the courage to invite Sally Mack to go to the pictures with him.

Sally knew that *Lorna Doone* starring Margaret Lockwood was showing in the Laurie Street Picture House and she was dying to see the film. She was also desperate to be asked by handsome Harry, but she was only fifteen, and what if he discovered that she was two inches smaller when she took off her high-heeled shoes? Throwing caution to the wind, she just nodded in agreement.

Harry had laughed to himself as he conceded that his mother taking Sally in when her mother had put her and her brother Peter out had ended up more to her advantage than to his. True, he had two clucking women looking after him, but they also had what they had both been lacking: a woman companion, and a strong, bonded mother-and-daughter relationship.

Harry vividly recalled standing in the Waverley Station on a sunny April day in 1940 hugging pregnant Sally. When he jumped aboard his mother called out, 'Off you go, son. And do your duty, and see Sally here...' She stopped, linked her arm through Sally's and continued, '...I'll look after her. No way would I let the lassie have her first bairn, my first grandchild, without me being with her every step of the road.'

The army had been good for Harry. It was there that his being able to sing had become an advantage: instead of being put on the front line he was seconded to kitchen duties and in his spare time he was expected to join the troupe that entertained the bored troops who were waiting to be sent overseas.

By the end of the war, Harry found settling down to civilian life difficult. He missed the camaraderie of the men and the dalliances with the pretty women. He always sighed and smiled when he thought of these flirtatious affairs. These women were so different to Sally. Sally was not as attractive, but she was safe. He always knew she would be there for him. Build his home. Have his children. Welcome his mother into their lives. And never would she complain. There was one problem though: Maggie. Maggie had become Sally's pal when Sally had gone to work in the Co-operative when Margo was a year old. Being five years older than Sally, Maggie had been a good help in settling Sally into the work routine. So it was only natural that they slipped into being pals who went to the pictures together. Before long, Maggie, who made Sally look beautiful, became part of the Stuart household.

Maggie had even been in the house the night Harry had come home to say he was now a fully trained train driver. And not only would he have his own train, but he had also been asked to sing at a workmen's club on Saturday night.

Throwing her arms around his neck, Sally chortled into his ear, 'You're joking.'

'I'm not,' replied Harry, disentangling himself from his heavily pregnant wife and giving her tummy an intimate pat. His eyes were now drawn to Maggie, whose expression made him feel uneasy, as if somehow he had no right to be demonstrating his affection for his wife.

Sally would always remember her mother's funeral in Seafield Crematorium as one of the weirdest she would ever attend in her life.

There were flowers and speeches, but no one except Josie cried. What Sally didn't know was that Josie wasn't crying because she had lost her mother, it was because her mother had deliberately kept her in the dark about Roy's mother's letters. Josie was so distraught she was unable to stand for the committal of the coffin. Her thoughts were away in America, where she was sure her life would have been so wonderful with her daughter and Roy's mother by her side.

Everyone returned to Iona Street for the boiled-ham tea. However, Sally felt spooked by her stepbrother Luke's behaviour when he took every opportunity to secretly indicate by dragging his fingers over his neck that he wished to cut Sally's throat. She had repeatedly told him that she hadn't stood by whilst Paddy ended their mother's life. But he had made up his mind that she had and, more importantly, that he would get even with her one day. This unreasonable behaviour resulted in Sally feeling she couldn't get out of the house quickly enough and therefore she and her family were first to leave.

On returning to Elgin Terrace, the tension of the day still hung heavily with Sally so she busied herself in the kitchen, but her thoughts were still in Iona Street. Attacking the potatoes with a peeler, she vowed she would never ever enter that house again. But then that would be easy because from the day she and Peter had been evicted from it she had detested the place.

Before she knew it, it was nine o'clock in the evening and she was sitting at the table drinking tea with Flora and Maggie, just idly chatting about nothing in particular, when Josie flounced in.

'Sally,' exclaimed Josie, flopping down on the settee, 'you're never going to believe this.'

Flora and Sally exchanged a knowing glance. Maggie's eyes flashed to the ceiling.

'Well,' continued Josie, apparently unaware of the reaction she was getting, 'I held on after you left. You know me: the skivvy who's always washing dishes and tidying up. But by five o'clock I'd had enough. Honestly, I just had to get out of there.'

Flora, Maggie and Sally all glanced at the clock before Sally asked, 'But it's gone ten; where have you been since five?'

'Walking...'

'You, walking?' exclaimed Flora, who knew that Josie walked very little because she always wore shoes whose heels were so high that she tottered.

Josie huffed. 'Yes: me, walking, because I was trying to get some sense into all that has happened these last few days.' She paused. 'And before I knew it,' she continued emphatically, 'I had joined the queue of the Palace Picture House in Constitution Street.'

'Surely you mean Duke Street,' Maggie was quick to suggest.

'No. If you go in the Duke Street queue it costs either one and sixpence or if you really want in straight away and a comfy seat then it's one and ninepence.'

'Oh, so you ended up standing in the one and three queue?'

'Yes, and that's where it all started to get unreal.' To her annoyance, her audience only glanced at each other and shrugged but no one verbally responded, so Josie babbled on. 'My mind was far away on the funeral and everything, but I became aware that there was now a restlessness in the crowd and people were nudging each other and whispering, "It is her. No one could mistake that face." I turned round to see who they were speaking about and the man behind me said, "It is you, isn't it? Wait until I tell my mates that there I was waiting to see James Mason in *A Star Is Born* and who else is in the queue wanting to see the film but none other than his previous co-star Margaret Lockwood!" Next thing they were all running to get bits of paper so I could give them my autograph.'

Flora rose to fill the kettle again. Maggie dropped her head and looked as if she was trying to pull her hair out. Sally sat dumbfounded whilst she wondered if Josie would ever stop these flights of fancy and get herself grounded in reality.

2

1960

'But, Mum,' twenty-year-old Margo protested, 'Annie Burgess, who just works gutting fish in Croan's factory, is having her wedding reception in the Assembly Rooms in Edinburgh.'

Sally wrinkled her brows and shrugged before suggesting, 'But surely you mean the Assembly Rooms in Leith.'

'No, Edinburgh. And that's because her granny, on her mother's side, is a Newhaven fishwife and she's contributing towards the festivities.'

She stood back to get a good look at her daughter, who, she conceded, was a better-looking woman than she was, but then Margo was taller than herself by six inches and had been fortunate enough to be endowed with the ginger-blonde locks of her father's people. The only assets Margo took from herself were her ability to speak up for herself and her crystal-blue eyes, which, somehow, like her late Granny Peggy's, lacked warmth.

Sally, who hated to be reminded of her mother, responded with a wry chuckle. 'Ah well, thankfully your grandmother, Peggy, on my side, has been keeping the good Lord company for five years now. And your other grandmother, Flora, has had to swallow her pride and take on the job of cleaning up every day in the Four Marys pub on the Shore in Leith.' Sally huffed before adding, 'And all because she let her nephew, William, sweet-talk her into him running her wee Highland croft for her.' Sally sighed before going on. 'Only problem with that is, he says he can't make a penny from it, so that means she has to stump up to pay the running costs.'

'So you're saying Granny won't be pitching in with any help for *my* wedding.'

'That's right. After she sends the money north this month to pay the rates on Culloden, she won't have enough left to help you finance the hiring of a telephone box.'

Sally wished she could be cruel enough to be truthful and also say, *And I might add that the thought of you and Johnny Souter, who haven't an ounce of common sense between you, getting married is the stuff of nightmares.*

Irritated by Sally's lack of enthusiasm, Margo spluttered, 'That's you all over, Mum. You're only happy when you're shooting my dreams down in flames.' Margo hesitated before adding, 'But this time there is a way for my aims to come true – whether you like it or not.'

'There is?'

Fearing retaliation from her mother, Margo waltzed around the table. 'Yes, and it's so simple.'

Simple, thought Sally. *Sometimes, my dear Margo, I think you are just that.*

Unaware that her mother was questioning her intelligence, Margo smiled affectedly before simpering, 'Yes. Now that Daddy has got a job on a Saturday night serenading the customers in the posh Albyn Rooms in Queen Street no less, that is where I should have my wedding.'

'As we are not related to Andrew Carnegie,' Sally managed to splutter through her laughter, 'where do you think we'll get the wherewithal to pay what they would charge?'

'Staff get a small discount,' Margo immediately retaliated.

'Sort of. But Maggie and I getting a buckshee dinner there on a busy Saturday night because we help clear up when the customers leave is very different to taking over the whole premises for the night.'

'I know that,' Margo protested. 'But as Daddy is so well in with the owner now...'

'Oh aye,' mocked Sally. 'None other than our gorgeous Ginny!'

'And,' Margo continued, ignoring her

mother's wry comment, 'if we agreed to have the wedding on a Monday, when the rooms are normally closed, it could all be done for the cost price of the food and a wee bung to the waiters and the band.' Margo's belief that she had at last outfoxed her astute mother was evident from the smug, self-satisfied expression on her face. 'So what do you have to say about all that?' she teased.

Dropping down on a chair, flabbergasted Sally found herself softly whistling as she drummed her fingers on her chin. She was grateful that Margo was keeping herself out of striking distance – not that Sally ever struck her children, but if ever she was to lose control and lash out at any of them, she knew it would be Margo. Shaking her head wearily, she reasoned that it was true that there were such things as idiosyncrasies running in families. *But*, she asked herself, *Why oh why does this child of mine have to take after my sister and suffer from delusions of grandeur? Surely, my good Lord, one bampot in a family is enough?*

'Mum, while you're in another of your trances I'm still waiting for an answer.'

'Mmm,' responded Sally, before eventually saying, 'know something, Margo, why don't you run your wonderful ideas past your dad.'

'I would, but as you know he has turned into the silent man these last six weeks.'

This statement came as a surprise to Sally,

who thought no one else had noticed the change in her Harry. *Know something,* she silently mused, *Never mind this blooming marriage between two young folk who are divorced from reality, I must get Dr Hannah to give my Harry the once-over.*

Two months later, the family assembled at the Church of Scotland's Pilrig/Dalmeny Church for the wedding of Margo to Johnny Souter.

Fifteen minutes had passed since Sally, accompanied by Flora, Josie and Maggie, had taken their seat in the front pew. Listening to the organ music should have calmed Sally, but she was engulfed by an atmosphere of dread. But then from the minute Margo had put her proposition to Harry, everything and everybody's attitude changed.

Sally conceded it was as if they had all become strangers. Maggie didn't seem comfortable visiting any more and she never suggested to her that they should go and see a picture in the Gateway Film House. Flora appeared worried about the expense the wedding was going to incur. To help with the cost she had badgered Ginny, who forby being the owner of the Albyn Rooms was also was the licensee of the Four Marys bar, to let her pull the pints there at lunchtime. And of course Ginny, who appeared to bend over backwards for Harry's relatives, immediately agreed. Josie – well, Josie kept herself busy with yet another male companion and when she was at home she kept mainly to her own basement flat.

Sally felt the problems had begun when Margo had sat herself down on her father's knee and begun twisting the lobe of his right ear. This was what she used to do when she was a child and she wished to bend Harry into giving in to her. But Margo was an adult now, so Sally had been shocked when Harry, without any further persuasion than a twist of his earlobe, agreed to ask Ginny about the hiring the Albyn Rooms. Drawing Margo closer into himself, he murmured, 'Look, Princess, your wish is my command.' Gently stroking her back, he whispered more to himself, 'And it's possible that in the future life will throw up some surprises that you could do without, so I'll just have to try to give you the lovely wedding day you will always remember.'

Sally recalled how Harry had then become quite emotional and avoided eye contact with herself and also his mother, who had just come home. Sally had long pondered that day. She knew what was ailing Harry was not physical. He had been thoroughly examined by Dr Hannah and given a clean bill of health. Maybe, she thought, it was just their firstborn Margo flying the nest that was getting to him. Sally shrugged. Or more likely that it was her refusal to ask Josie to give up the basement flat so that Margo could move in when she married.

Why couldn't they understand, she wondered, *that for me to have put out Josie would reinforce the feelings of rejection that Josie has felt all her life. True, she lives in cloud cuckoo land, but how else could she have survived the abusive childhood she had endured if she had not had a means of escape?* Sally sniffed back her tears. *And after all, it could be the making of over-indulged Margo when she has to live in a cramped bedroom at her mother-in-law's guddle of a house. But then rumour has it that Ella Souter, who had been widowed by the war, is a gallus, accommodating lady – but hasn't sunk as far as the ladies of the night who frequent the Four Marys bar to make a living – no, she is more a 'must be at a party every night' and 'new lover every season'.*

With bile rising in her throat, Sally finally recalled how she was forced to concede that Margo's wedding would be a day to remember. This had come about when only a week after Harry had given his promise to Margo he had breezed in and, doing a jig around the room, announced that his darling daughter would not only drive in state from the church to the Albyn Rooms on her wedding day, but instead of it being on a Monday hadn't Ginny offered to accommodate them on a Saturday. This statement not only astonished Sally but caused her sleepless nights, wondering why Ginny was being so benevolent.

Margo had insisted that Bobby, her thirteen-year-old brother, be her chief usher, whilst relegating her fourteen-year-old sister, Helen, from bridesmaid to flower girl. The reasoning behind this was that Margo thought Helen, whom she considered to be less attractive than herself, had what her granny called 'a gift from the gods' – charisma – so she was afraid her younger sister would take attention away from her. Sally was still reminiscing about this when she felt a touch on her arm.

Looking up into Bobby's green eyes, she was pleased that everyone in attendance would be able to see how he resembled his dad. He had Harry's athletic build – true, his hair was fairer than Harry's, but it did have the same curly kinks. She smiled when she remembered that only yesterday he had told her that having to have your shoes built up was all the rage now. Even his pal, Ron, had bought some platform-soled shoes – in Ron's case it was to make him seem taller than his five feet three inches. 'Mum, are you listening to me?' Sally nodded when she realised he was asking her to accompany him to the back of the church. Rising to follow him, she became aware that throughout the congregation a whispering had started – she knew they were speculating as to why she had been summoned.

As the click-click-clicking of her heels echoed ominously on the church floor, she felt panic rising in her breast. *What is wrong? Has Margo at last come to her senses and decided that life with the Souters won't suit her? Or, more likely…?* Now she had allowed her fertile imagination to take control, Sally found herself breaking into a run for the last few yards. This was because she now believed the problem wasn't with Margo but with Harry! *Oh yes*, she screamed inwardly, *Dr Hannah was wrong when he advised me that Harry was as fit as a fiddle and now … and now. Oh no, please God, don't let him be like his father and die long before his time.*

Bolting through the doors and into the vestibule, a tearful Sally stopped abruptly before sinking against the wall. Relief seeped in. Thankfully Harry was standing beside Margo. Sally thought he had never looked more handsome and debonair. The greying of his hair at the temples gave him an air of sophistication, and somehow he had thrived on the wedding preparations and lately he had walked with an air of confidence – unlike herself, who was consumed by a feeling of impending disaster.

'Mum, look at me,' Margo pleaded. 'What do you think? Will I do? And Mum, what if I'm not doing the right thing?'

Sally looked to Harry for guidance, but he deliberately turned his gaze away. *But then, she asked herself, has he ever taken any of the awkward family decisions? No.*

Drawing on the inner strength that up till now had never failed her, Sally took Margo's hand in hers. 'My darling child,' she murmured, 'without a doubt you are the most beautiful bride I have ever seen. And know something else?' Dropping Margo's hand, Sally now stepped back to get a full view of her daughter. 'The dress and the veil,' she mused, 'I now admit are worth every penny. Oh aye, a right royal princess you look.' Drawing Margo into an embrace, Sally then whispered in her ear, 'So come on, girl, don't you disappoint your audience. Go in there and knock them dead.' Then to herself she said, *And don't you worry, if marrying Johnny Souter is the wrong thing for you, which I fear it might be, just come back home and I'll arrange a divorce – quite the fashionable thing to do these days so I'm told.*

It came as a surprise to Sally that the wedding, with such diverse guests, was an outstanding success. She knew the meal provided by the Albyn chefs would be something most guests would savour and talk about for weeks to come. The only complaint about the food came from Margo's new mother-in-law. Ella, who gave the impression she was truly upstairs when in reality the deluded soul had never got her foot above the first step, had asked in a voice that could be heard at the foot of Leith Walk, 'Why have we been served half-cooked sirloin steaks, crème caramels and coffee in ridiculous wee cups when everybody with an ounce of breeding kens it's steak pie, sherry trifle and a cup of strong Lipton's tea that is served up at decent weddings?'

The night had progressed into a typical good Leith knees-up. The Master of Ceremonies knew his job. He had expertly judged the guests and therefore the dances were mainly waltzes and Scottish reels. For the first dance after the bride and groom and their attendants had taken the floor, Harry bowed to Ella before steering her onto the floor. The second dance he should have had with Sally, but as he progressed over the floor towards her, Ginny jumped in front of Sally and Maggie and said, 'Oh now Harry, how did you know my favourite dance is a Gay Gordons, especially when I'm asked up by a handsome, debonair man?' Embarrassed at being wrong-footed, all Sally could do was to start fulfilling her hostess duties. Fixing a smile on her face, she called at each table and thanked everybody individually for coming and sharing the family's happy day.

No one, not even Ella, could say they did

not enjoy the festivities, and when Harry got up to serenade the assembly he had to wait for two minutes until the applause stopped. However, instead of starting straight into his song, Sally felt a lump rise in her throat when he went over to Margo, who had now changed into her going-away outfit, and taking her hand in his he began to sing, 'I'm Walking Behind You on Your Wedding Day'.

It was just after one o'clock in the morning when Sally, Flora, Helen, Bobby and Josie got home. Poor Harry had bundled them into a taxi, but he had to wait behind mainly because he said he would have to help the staff with the tidying up but beside that five was the limit for travellers in a taxi.

Harry was surprised when he arrived home at four o'clock that Sally was still waiting up for him. She had felt that she had to spend some time with him. After all, it had been a big day for them – their firstborn becoming a married woman. Sally smiled as she remembered that even although they had been together all day they never had seemed to find time to talk to each other. That was because her Harry, being the perfect host that he was, had spent all his time making sure everybody was enjoying the party. He had been so busy he hadn't even found time to dance with her.

Setting himself down on a chair opposite Sally, Harry drawled, 'It never occurred to me that you would still be up.'

Rising to go over and sit on Harry's knee, Sally chuckled, thinking back to the old days when he would slap his knees as a signal that he wished her to jump up on his lap. However, the sound died in her throat when Harry arose and brushed past her. 'Sally,' he said, 'now we are alone I think we should get some things straight.'

'Straight? What do you mean?'

'Just... Look... We have to talk. You have to understand.'

'Understand what?'

'The way things are changing – or to be truthful – how they have, slowly over the years, changed between us.'

Sally gave a nervous little twitter. 'Of course things change. Nothing stays the same, but you and I, Harry, we've grown in strength and our love...'

'That's just it, Sally, our love for each other is past tense. I cannot remember the last time you said you loved me and we slept like two spoons.'

This statement to Sally was so cruel that at first she decided not to answer it, but then she found herself quietly saying, 'When the word "love" is spoken it means nothing. You see, when you love someone you don't have to tell them every day – well, not if they are adult – they know you love them by all that you do for them. Like giving birth to their children, keeping their house, loving their mother as your own, nursing them when they're sick. Oh yes, and love is patient, it does not fly into rages...'

Harry had listened enough. 'Look, Sally, your guff has no influence on me. What I want is for you to love me enough to let me go. Give me a divorce!'

Sally started to whine like an injured puppy dog, but even her pitiful cries couldn't stop him wounding her further.

'Don't you realise,' he ruthlessly continued, 'I wish to be free to marry someone who makes me feel like you used to. She is without a doubt the love of my life now.'

Pressing her hands over her lips Sally tried to hush the terror-stricken screams that were rising in her throat. Although there was silence for only a minute between Harry and she, it seemed like an eternity. Eventually she managed to mumble, 'Harry, you don't know what you're saying. You're having a mid-life crisis or something.' Her right hand swept around the room to add emphasis to her plea. 'Look, really look, at what we have built up here. This is not only *our* home: it is our children's, your mother's, my sister's place of safety – a place where they know they are loved and wanted.'

With a shake of his head and a wry contortion of his mouth, Harry snorted, 'You still don't see it, do you? This...' he now indicated with a backward jerk of his thumb, '...is where all your lame ducks are welcomed. But me – for years I've realised that I'm just the one who goes out to two jobs to earn the money to keep them all in the comfort that they now think they are entitled to – but for no longer. Tomorrow I'm off into the arms of someone who thinks I'm the whole cheese and not just the smell.'

Sally felt as if she was in a nightmare from which she must escape, so she picked up the loose skin of her left hand and pinched it so severely she howled, but still she didn't awaken. 'But Harry,' she heard herself saying, 'if you go I won't be able to pay the mortgage and we, that is our Helen, Bobby and your mother, will all become homeless.'

'And I hope you don't think with the way you have indifferently treated me these last few years that that will change my mind. Listen again, but this time listen good. I am leaving you – I need a speedy divorce. So I am going to make you an offer that you would be foolish to refuse.' Harry, who seemed oblivious to Sally's utter distress, continued. 'As you are aware, I am listed as the owner of this house here, so this is my over-generous proposal: everybody residing in the house is to vacate it within fourteen days. I will then immediately put it up for sale and provided you don't give me any further grief I will give you, and take note I do not require to do so, 50 per cent of the selling price.'

Picking the bread knife up from the table, Sally leapt in front of Harry. 'You unfeeling bastard,' she screamed. 'Have you taken leave of your senses or something?'

Sheer panic gripped Harry and he became mesmerised as the brandished blade came ever closer and closer to his face. Gulping and gasping, he kept swerving away in an effort to defend himself. Ashen-faced and buckling at the knees, with great effort he managed to splutter. 'N-o-o-o. Not lost my senses – j-j-j-j-just come to them.'

'That right,' Sally screeched as she endeavoured again to slash at Harry's face. 'Well, if you think you can get away with this then think again. Oh aye, and have you thought what people will say about you not only flinging me and your kids out onto the street but also your very own mother?' Sally felt someone at her back wresting the knife from her. Turning, she came face to face with Flora. Spinning round to face Harry again, she spat, 'Look at her, Harry. See what the years of going out to scrub and clean to get a bob or two to help us get by has done to her.'

Drawing Sally into an embrace and tossing the knife into the fireplace, Flora, her face contorted with grief and anger, then looked at her son and he was left in no doubt about the contempt in which she held him. 'So, fornicating coward that you are,' she sobbed, 'you have at last told her about your scandalous, sordid affair – and with someone whom she had given houseroom to because nobody else would.'

'Mum, you know I cannot make you homeless. You have a house in Smithton. A house that is big enough for you, Sally and the bairns. You could even give room to...'

Sally was so distraught she hadn't at first comprehended that a person close to her was his paramour. Breaking free from Flora's arms, Sally fled towards the basement flat to confront Josie.

Throwing open the door and bounding down the steps, she kicked open the door to Josie's bedroom. It had been her intention to drag Josie from her bed, but Josie was not abed. She was standing up dressed in her outdoor clothing, hands clapped over her ears and weeping profusely. Being younger and therefore more agile than Sally, Josie sprang up on the bed when she became aware that her sister was out of control and that she could be on the receiving end of her wrath.

'Come here, you man-mad bitch,' screeched Sally while she attempted to grab hold of Josie. 'How many times have I told you not get entangled with married men?

How many times have I had to sort out your problems?'

Josie did try desperately to find the right words to placate Sally, but she could think of nothing. Sally was about to leap onto the bed beside her when Flora entered. 'Sally, why are you trying to attack Josie?'

'I'll tell you why,' was Sally's hysterical response, 'because she has stolen my husband's love and he wants to leave me and our bairns for her – bloody hoor is what she is.'

Flora managed to get herself in between Josie and Sally. Without warning, she smacked Sally firmly on the face. The act of violence, as Sally saw it, caused her to sink to the floor, and sobs racked her body. 'Och, lassie,' Flora began, 'your feckless sister is not the harlot who has her claws into Harry. Sure, when she discovered what was going on between Harry and that wanton Jezebel, like me, all she did wrong was to try to shield you from the truth. Hoped in vain, the both of us did, that sanity would return to him but...' Flora paused as she became aware that Josie was becoming quite hysterical and required comforting. Going over to her, Flora took her in her arms. 'There, there,' she murmured while gently stroking her back. Agonising minutes elapsed before Flora had Josie suitably composed. Holding on to each other, both women looked for Sally, but she was nowhere to be seen.

Fearing that she had returned to the main house to inflict a fatal injury on Harry, they now sped back up the stairs into the living room only to find Sally's coat and handbag were gone, as was Harry.

Scampering like a scared rabbit, Sally emerged into Easter Road when, as luck would have it, a taxi drew up to let a passenger alight. Before the driver could put up his flag to signal he was for hire, Sally was in the back of the cab. 'Albyn Rooms in Queen Street, driver,' Sally instructed before she was asked for a destination.

'Sure they'll have been locked up for hours.'

'I'm not really going to the rooms. You see, I've been invited by the owner to her penthouse flat for a meeting.'

The driver found the explanation about a meeting at four o'clock in the morning a bit odd, but he pushed down the flag and drove off in the direction of Queen Street.

Having settled up with the taxi driver, Sally alighted from the taxi and she was just about to ring the bell when the door opened and a suave, debonair, titled gentleman who she recognised stepped out. Lifting his Anthony Eden hat to Sally, he said, 'Lovely morning. Sun will soon be up, but not, I fear, dear Ginny if it is she you wish to visit.'

Making no comment, Sally crossed over the threshold and without an invitation she ran up the stairs and barged into the flat and then the master bedroom.

The banging of the door off the wall startled Ginny and she sprang up into a sitting position. 'Don't tell me you've forgotten something, Billy boy,' she asked whilst drawing the bedcovers further up over herself. 'I did warn you that I am happy to have you share a nightcap with me, but I never – ever – share my bed with any *married* man.'

'That right?' Sally sarcastically responded.

Ginny arose from the bed. 'Thought I might get a visit from you,' she said, lifting her dressing gown and enveloping herself in it before looking at the clock, 'but not at this unearthly hour.

'So the louse has told you,' she said as she sat down on the edge of the bed.

'If you mean he's announced he's about to leave me and sell my home from under my feet so that he can come to you with the necessary collateral, then...'

Uncontrollable laughter from Ginny stopped Sally from going on.

'So you think it's funny gutting another woman, do you?'

'No, Sally, I don't. And as to Harry... Well, he may be able to warble a good tune but not dulcet enough for me. You see, I do not wish to offend you, but I wouldn't have an affair with your husband – he's on the slide now and the next ring that goes on my finger will come along with pots of dough and maybe, not necessarily though, a title thrown in. Lady Ginny has a nice ring to it. Wouldn't you say?'

Sally couldn't say anything. Had she got it wrong again? Feeling quite faint, she slumped down on the bed beside Ginny. 'But you were the one who grabbed him for the second dance and you knew he was coming for me. Do you realise how humiliated I felt when you did that?'

'Believe me, if I'd let him take up that conniving cow... Humiliation – that can be coped with. But what both of them had planned for you was for the whole assembly to see you crushed and beaten.' Shaking her head, Ginny then put her hand over Sally's. 'You had no idea?'

Drained Sally could only shake her head.

'Didn't you see what was going on under your nose?' Ginny continued.

'No. And even now I haven't got a clue. I just know he's leaving me for someone I counted as ... a friend.'

'Then think. Really think. Who was there?'

'You, Josie, Flora... a-a-a-and...' Sally paused before adding. '*Maggie*... Oh no,' she sobbed, 'not my bosom pal, Maggie!'

Ginny could only nod her head before saying, 'None other than.'

'But I am the only person who has ever given her the time of day. I felt sorry for her. I pitied her. I invited her into my home and made her welcome.'

'And Jezebel that she is ... she has repaid you by stealing your man.'

'But if you knew all that, why did you give us the rooms and all we required for Margo's wedding for just the cost of the food?'

'Mistakenly, I thought that when you were all here as a family enjoying Margo's wedding he would appreciate all that he had. Think twice about throwing away the gold and picking up the dross.'

Sally half turned herself towards Ginny. 'You did all that for my family but mostly myself... Why?'

A long minute ticked by before Ginny replied, 'Everybody thinks I have it all. Did have once,' she chuckled. 'But a blue-eyed blonde fourteen years younger than me with legs that went on forever came along and, bingo, she poached my preserve. Now I accept I was luckier than you because I got sympathy for being ousted by a nubile twenty-five-year-old, whereas...' she stopped to pick her words carefully but decided that truth was best and added, '...you have had the added ignominy of being replaced by an ugly older bitch.'

Sally ignored Ginny's truthful comments on Maggie. 'But you seem,' she began quietly, 'to be quite wealthy and readjusted.'

'Seem. And right enough I was astute enough to get a good settlement out of him, which I used to start up my businesses. But the blow to my confidence and esteem when he dumped me...' She now patted her left shoulder, 'still haunts me and is responsible for this big chip on my shoulder.'

Sally nodded. 'I'm different from you. Any settlement I get will be needed for a deposit on a house – that's if they now give mort-gages to women. I have no talent for getting a business up and running.' Sally looked at herself in the dressing table mirror. Ner-vously, she stoked her hair before saying, 'I'm just about to say hello to my forties – so what have I got going for me?'

Ginny seemed deep in thought and Sally was surprised when she eventually said, 'Look at the time. It's nearly six o'clock.' She arose from the bed before announcing, 'It's breakfast time. So how about you and I nipping up to the Caledonian Hotel to have a good old Scottish breakfast and then I'll send you home in a taxi?'

'I can't. I'm too upset. You see, I don't know what to do. Be reasonable, how can I eat bacon and eggs when I don't know what's going to happen to my children, Flora and Josie?'

'Well, if you persist in feeling sorry for your-self they'll end up in the gutter. But if you get

106

up off your backside and start putting up a fight, and I'll hold your coat while you're doing it, you'll be surprised at what a woman on her own can achieve.'

Sally arrived home just before lunch and when she entered the living room she was confronted by her broken-hearted daughter Helen, her irate son Bobby, her embarrassed mother-in-law and Josie, who was trying to give the impression that she had led a blameless life and therefore she'd felt gutted that Sally could think she would be the type of person who would lead on her sister's man and break up her home.

Knowing that she owed a lot to Flora, Sally decided to speak to her first. 'Look, *Mum*,' she said, deliberately using the term 'Mum' with emphasis so Flora could be left in no doubt about how much she loved her. 'It is true Harry has left us – all of us – and we must leave here.' Sally's eyes became moist and she looked around the room that had known all of them and their so many happy times. 'However, don't panic. Ginny Strang has spent time talking to me and if we all put our shoulder to the wheel we will survive.'

'So you are not going to beg Dad to come back?' whimpered Helen.

'No she's no,' Bobby answered for her. 'If he wants to leave us for a zombie then just leave him to it.' He turned to directly face Sally. 'And tell him, Mum, that when he wakes up one morning and finds out he's made one hell'ova mistake no to knock on our door!'

This statement rattled Sally. She still loved Harry ... still thought of him as her ever-loving husband and caring father of her children. But how could she say to everybody here that she knew that if he did ever knock on the door and ask her to take him back she would welcome him in? Deciding not to say any more on the subject, she changed the topic and lightly announced, 'Good news is, we'll all be moving back to Leith.' Sally looked directly at Josie when she explained, 'But we won't all be living together. Josie, you'll have a wee flat of your own, and Mum, you, the bairns and me will be together.' They all looked from one to the other and were aghast when Sally concluded with, 'And we won't starve: you see, Ginny is going to train me and then give me a job as a barmaid!'

Later on when she was alone in the house, Sally congratulated herself on having every-one believe that she was able to sort things out and that they would all be going with her.

In truth, she was terrified of what life now held for her. The major problem wasn't the fact she that she would be holding down a full-time job that she had no experience of.

Sighing, she thought, *If only that was the major obstacle*. Reluctantly she acknowledged that what was really causing her intolerable anguish was her having to accept that she was now deprived of Harry's love and companionship. Since she was just a strip of a girl of sixteen years, he had been her rock to cling to. Now she had been traded in for an older model. Gentle tears spilled down her face as she wished just to be able to touch his hand and drift off to sleep to the peaceful rhythm of his snoring.

In addition to her being deprived of him, there was the problem of taking Josie down into the heart of the seedier part of Leith. Josie was very fond of male company, but she had never been exposed to women who made a living from degrading themselves.

Getting on with life and dragging her children, Flora and Josie seemed to be too large a task for her right now. She concluded she needed to escape, like she had done as a child when life with her mother had been intolerable – flee back into her private dream world; however, this time not with a doting mother but with Harry.

Sally accepted that her function in life now was, or to be truthful would continue to be, looking after all those who needed her. Rising to make a cup tea, she closed her weary eyes when she passed the mirror – she just didn't wish to see the fear and despair in them.

She had just sat down to enjoy the newly brewed tea when footsteps in the hall alerted her. Looking up expectantly, she was surprised when Harry, suitcase in hand, walked in.

Trying to keep her hopes from soaring, she looked at the suitcase and then Harry before sarcastically saying, 'Don't tell me you've come crawling back already?'

Harry let the case slip from his grip and as it hit the floor the hollow sound told her it was empty. 'No. Just come for some more of my stuff. And to thank you,' he replied in a voice laden with irony.

Taking another sip from her tea, Sally deliberately allowed time to tick by.

'Yeah,' Harry continued with a derisive grimace, 'thank you for getting me the sack from the Albyn.'

'What?' Sally exclaimed. 'If you did get your books the only one to blame is ... yourself!'

Harry's contemptuous laughter echoed throughout the room. 'You know something, Sally, I never saw you for what you are until Maggie pointed it out to me.'

'Oh, the gospel according to St Maggie is what straightened you out?'

'Aye, and a good life the two of us are going to have. Two people who have been made mugs of starting to grab a life for themselves. Mind you, I have to hand it to you Sally, I never dreamt for a minute that the wee mouse that you portray yourself as could persuade a hard nut like Ginny to say goodbye to her Saturday night's best advert. You must have something on her.'

'Believe what you like, Harry. I don't give a monkey's uncle what you or Maggie think.'

'Right. The only things left now to settle between us are my access to Helen and Bobby and getting the house up for sale.'

'Thought you knew all about the house and it was all yours? You, like me, have seen a solicitor?' she lied. He nodded. 'Then you'll know I am entitled to a half share. It's funny how we never pay attention to laws being changed until it suits us. Thank goodness Ginny is up to the minute in the law. So that means I'll be taking one month, and a calendar one at that, to move out, and it will be me who shows the house to prospective buyers.' She paused before drawling, 'As to Helen and Bobby, they have said they wished you were dead and they will not visit you and your ugly...'

'Sally, you don't get it, do you? Maggie may be plain to you, but I love her and to me she is not only beautiful inside but also outside.'

Exactly five days after her wedding, Margo bounced into the house. 'Hello, Mum, I'm just back,' she crooned, 'but I just had to come and see Dad and you straight away. Have to thank you again for my wonderful day. Remember it? I sure will my whole life through.'

Sally silently agreed that it was a day that the whole family would forever remember – but for many different reasons. She didn't wish to speak to her daughter because how could she tell her the truth about her father? Margo had always held him in such high regard – put him on a pedestal. Reluctantly, Sally acknowledged she would have to say something and she was surprised to hear herself ask, 'Where's Johnny?'

'Sent him, I did, on to his mother with our luggage. Oh Mum, what a fantastic honeymoon I've had. And okay, it was only five days in a bed and breakfast in Dunbar, unlike Annie, whose Auntie June, another fishwife, paid for them to have a fortnight in Lloret de Mar, no less...' Margo stopped to add emphasis, '...but *my* darling Johnny was so loving and attentive to me I forgot to be jealous of Annie. And I know how we feel about each other will last forever.'

Sally nodded before saying, in a fatigued, laden, uninterested voice, 'Glad you had a good time, dear.'

Her mother's lack of enthusiasm caused Margo to look questioningly not only at her mother, but also around the room. The floor in front of her was littered with packing cases and cardboard boxes. Her eyes then took in her grandmother, Flora, who was sitting in the corner carefully wrapping up Sally's best china in newspapers.

'Oh Mum, you and Dad are moving to a bigger house,' Margo exclaimed. Thinking that her parents were buying a bigger house so they could take in Johnny and herself to live with them, she rattled on, 'Isn't that just so like my dad to go out of his way to keep us all together?'

'Aye,' Sally replied, 'we're moving right enough, but not with your dad because ... he's already moved out and is now kipping up with his girlfriend. So that means this house, our dear home, is up for sale and the rest of us, including your granny, his very own mother, are being thrown out.'

'You have to be joking,' Margo gasped, looking towards Flora, who nodded her head.

'Sorry, lass, I find it hard to believe myself, but what your mother says is true. Had the nerve to give us notice to quit and we'll all be out of here within days. But, as ever, your mother had come up trumps and she's found us a flat to rent at 68 Great Junction Street, in Leith.'

Margo started to pace up and down like a caged animal. After three agonising minutes, she spluttered, 'Let me get this straight –

Dad has a girlfriend – and who exactly would that be?'

'None other than my good *old* pal, Maggie,' Sally retorted.

'Aaaah, now it makes sense. And do you know, Mum, this is your entire fault?'

'My fault?' yelled Sally.

'Yes, because whenever Dad came in you were conveniently out and Maggie danced attendance on him. Often I came in and she was whisking him up an omelette or heating him some soup she had made herself. And more importantly, whenever he was doing a gig she was there to cheer him on. When did you ever spend time applauding his efforts? Poor Dad. Imagine him being so desperate that he had to find love and comfort in a doormat like Maggie.'

3

Two weeks later, whilst walking through Leith Links for her first day at the Four Marys bar, Sally was reminded that Leith was a strong, vibrant, supportive community. Never could you be on the links or streets that you wouldn't meet someone who would pass the time of day with you.

She smiled as she acknowledged the waves

of a woman hanging up her washing on the drying greens, but then it was a warm, sunny day, therefore the women of Leith would think it wasteful not to use the gift. Sally then remembered that the women hung their washing there because their homes were small and cramped so there was nowhere really to hang up a dish towel never mind a full washing.

Loud banging caused her to halt and look over towards the old town. Like herself, the ancient houses, shops, homeless hostels, businesses and old cobbled streets of the Kirkgate, Tolbooth Wynd and all their surrounding areas were being smashed to pieces in the mistaken belief that the change from the old, comforting and beneficial order was needed.

Sally allowed a short, contemptuous laugh to escape her. *I wonder*, she thought, *if those sitting up in the City Chambers in Edinburgh High Street, who have deemed that the houses, shops and streets that have known so many people and so much history are no longer fit for the purpose, have really thought through the consequences of their rash actions? Would these,* she further mused, *faceless City Fathers ever accept that Leithers, like myself consider the demolitions acts of pure vandalism. Don't they see that as they tear out the heart of old Leith they are also breaking the hearts of the people?* She chuckled again when she considered the proposals of building multi-storeyed flats that the Leith people, who had been temporarily rehoused in all the airts, would inhabit. Sally made a bet with herself that in years to come the magnificent rebuilding of the Old Fort slum area would itself be deemed 'unfit'. *Oh yes*, she almost shouted. *You can take the people out of Leith, but you'll never ever take Leith out of the people!*

'Time to move on,' she said to herself, but she knew she would take a while to arrive at the Four Marys because she would stop at the Old Court House, now the Leith Police Station, to admire the magnificence of the building but more importantly to pray that the sadistic childhood that her brother Peter, her sister Josie and herself had known would never have to be endured by any other bairns – especially the birching Peter had endured. She would then move on to appreciate the magnificent buildings in Constitution Street and Bernard Street.

These buildings had been erected when independent Leith was proud and prosperous and the envy of Edinburgh: covetous Edinburgh, who had in 1920, against the will of the people of Leith, forced upon them the amalgamation with themselves... After that disastrous decision should they not reconsider what they were proposing and doing to Leith today? After all, the ancient port had had, until the wreckers moved in, some of the oldest streets in the whole of Scotland. So why didn't they listen to those who said that the facades should be preserved and the houses and shops upgraded – didn't they see what a tourist boon that would be? Imagine it: people from all over the world flocking to Leith to enjoy the architecture and see a way of life that was long gone.

By the time she had stopped raving to herself about the myopic planners she was at the pend in Bernard Street that gave you access to the houses above the two pubs on the Shore. Even although the entrance was in Bernard Street, the windows of the flats overlooked the Water of Leith on the Shore.

True, the houses were ancient and in sore need of renovation to bring them up to habitable standard. But Sally smiled, as she willingly believed the rumour that as a matter of urgency it was planned to upgrade and modernise the houses and pubs.

However, she had to accept that that expediency, to the powers that be, could mean within ten years. This stark realisation set Sally pondering about the state of the houses today. She shuddered. Would anyone appreciate that when she was a child she had lived in such a house in Ferrier Street, which you approached through the hole in the wall in Leith Walk?

Relaxing slightly, she recalled that when they had been allocated the house in Iona

Street she had thought that never again would she or any of her family have to live in such squalor.

The flat that Ginny was renting to Josie at a nominal rent belonged to whoever was the licensee of the Four Marys pub – in this case Ginny – who also held the licence for the adjacent pub, the King's Wark. It was obvious both hostelries had at one time been a solitary establishment.

Sally began to argue with herself again, but, no matter what, she had to accept that this was the abode that Josie would be required to move into. It was true Ginny had done her best to revamp the place. She had had the walls painted, and had laid new linoleum and even rugs upon the floors of the two-roomed house, but even she could do nothing to upgrade one cold-water tap and an outside lavatory.

Getting into the Four Marys pub on time should have been Sally's priority, but she was detained by wondering how Josie would feel about going through these rusty iron gates before entering into the dark, dank, eerie courtyard and then climbing the ancient, crumbling, worn stairs?

If only, Sally prayed, *Josie can hold on until the promised upgrading is carried out, which will mean the knocking of two houses into one and installing modern facilities in the form of hot water and a bathroom. She will be in a good position to be considered as a tenant for one of them.*

Sheer panic started to rise in Sally's breast until she reluctantly remembered that Flora had said it was time Josie was standing on her own two feet and her moving into a flat on her own could be the start. Sally exhaled forcibly as she admitted to herself that as far as she could she had always sheltered Josie from the cruelties and realities of life, but now she had to give all her support to Helen and Bobby, who had been so ruthlessly abandoned by their father. Sighing, she thought, *Yes, it is about time thirty-one-year-old Josie is responsible for herself, and there is no reason that she cannot do more to make the flat as comfortable as possible.*

Sally remonstrated with herself before she continued, *I know what I'll do to have Josie know I still care for her – I'll buy her a commode so she won't need to go downstairs at night to use the outside lavatory.* She convinced herself that she had come up with a brilliant idea to protect Josie – because there was the possibility, in the dark, that she could be mistaken for an accommodating lady of the ancient King's Wark and find that instead of relieving herself she had been propositioned. Sally gave a wicked little chuckle as she conceded that would never do.

It didn't take much imagination when you looked straight on at the front of the Four

Marys and the King's Wark pubs to accept that once they had been the same building.

Sally smiled as she remembered when as a child how she had been given history lessons, which always included the details of what the building that now housed the two pubs had been used for.

She chuckled as she acknowledged that there was not one bairn in Leith who didn't know that in 1575 those suffering from the dreaded plague were treated in the building, which had been turned into a hospital. The children also shared stories about the ghostly appearances of people who lurked in the great cellar that ran underneath both establishments. These boggies had either died of the plague or had been burned to death when the Wark was destroyed by fire in the 1690s.

During the following years, the building had many renovations to suit the several changes of use it experienced. It was during one of these alterations that the two hostelries came into being.

Sally wondered when the first customers had drunk fine wine from silver tankards if they imagined over the centuries that both establishments would be known infamously throughout the whole wide modern world as the Jungle.

Could they have imagined that all that would remain of the royal patronage they had enjoyed were the names – the King's Wark and the Four Marys? And what would they say about the gallus women who made their living by accommodating sailors of all nationalities and therefore brought world-wide notoriety to the hostelries? Until recently, every night in these establishments fallen women had bedded men for a few bob, which they then spent on Red Biddy, a cheap, harsh wine. It would be a funny night that the Leith police were not called in to break up fights, not only between men but also women. These women were also expert at getting their clients so drunk that they were then able to rob them before eventually pushing them out into the gutter to sleep it off.

That was what life in the Jungle had been like, but Ginny, a shrewd businesswoman who was always looking at changing trends, had decided that Leith pubs would need to transform if they were to survive. It was also true that the Leith constabulary had warned her when she took over the pubs that change was necessary and if it was not forthcoming then the establishments would be closed down. What they were actually saying was that no longer could they turn a blind eye to the sordid businesses that were carried out under their noses.

Ginny had noted not only that men would no longer be able to seek out the comfort of a woman in pubs, she had also realised that long gone were the days when a man walked into a pub on payday and staggered out to hand over the pittance of what was left to his wife, who would then have to work a miracle to be able to feed and clothe her bairns. Since the war there had been great social changes, especially in the attitude of working-class women. Not only was there now the blessed welfare state, but women also knew that they were not wholly financially dependent on any man and they were therefore able to stand up for their rights to be equal in the marriage deal. They also wished to have nights out at the pictures and perhaps be taken afterwards for a wee sherry or what were becoming the must-have drinks – a Pimm's No. 1 ora brandy and Babycham. Then there was the unthinkable: before the war, a woman would be happy to stay at home and have numerous children, but now she was better educated and because of the contraceptive pill she was in charge of the decision as to when she would have children and how many.

This being the case, pubs would need to change to become places where men would wish to take their wives out for the evening and where women would feel safe and comfortable.

Sally, with Ginny's words still echoing in her mind, decided she'd have to get a move on and get herself into the Four Marys. Dancing over the cobbles, she noted that the building had been erected centuries ago and she wondered how the stonemasons, who'd have been without all the assistance that craftsmen had today, had managed to erect these buildings out of solid hewn stones.

Sniffing and nodding, she opened the door thinking that long after she and her children would be no more, this substantial building would still be standing.

If the outside of the building was a reminder of how hard the tradesmen had worked when Leith was a prosperous town in its own right then the inside carried on the illusion. The bar, which dominated the room, was constructed from oak, and in the firelight its polished lustre gleamed. Last week there had been a sawdust trough around the outside floor of the bar. This was where pipe-smoking men spat into – 'Disgusting habit,' Ginny had declared – and now a gleaming brass foot-rail had replaced it, and if you didn't like it then Ginny thought you should take yourself up to the Standard Bar on the broad pavement where Myles Dolan still provided Red Biddy for fallen women and spittoons for drunken men.

From the very small kitchen a young woman called, 'We're no open yet. Eleven o'clock is when our licence allows us to serve drink.'

'I'm not wanting a drink – well, not of alcohol, though I could murder a cup of tea.'

Immediately the woman, who was drying her hands on a tea towel, emerged from the cubbyhole. 'You Sally?'

'Yeah,' Sally replied. 'And you must be, Rita. My mother-in-law has told me all about you.'

Rita scratched the side of her head, sought in her apron pocket and brought out a packet of Player's cigarettes, from which she took one. Advancing to the fire, she selected a wax taper, which she then placed in the flames before using it to light her cigarette. Blowing out the flickering flame of the taper, she turned slowly back towards Sally.

Both women were now eyeing each other up. Sally accepted that it must be humiliating for Rita to have to accept that Ginny was going to groom herself to run this pub and bring it up to the standard she wished.

However, Sally was totally wrong in thinking that Rita was crushed by her arrival. On the contrary, Rita had found it difficult not to cheer when diminutive Sally walked in. Never in her life had she seen someone quite so unsuitable to be a barmaid in Leith. The poor soul, as Rita saw Sally, was not only on the short side to square up to a drunken man but she also appeared too ladylike to hauckle any belligerent hag towards the door. Rita had to stifle a sly snigger when she pictured short-statured Sally dealing with the Four Marys' self-appointed madam – none other than big, bellicose Nancy Greenfield. Rita vowed there and then that the meeting between those two women was something she just couldn't miss. After all, it would end in what Rita wished to see: Sally falling flat on her face. On the other hand, glancing at Sally's ample bosom Rita was forced to acknowledge that with her having been endowed with a bust that would be the envy of Marilyn Monroe, if ever she did fall over she would bounce straight back up.

Deciding that it would be best to try and break the ice with Rita, Sally sweetly smiled before suggesting, 'How about you and I have a cup of tea, then you can take me down to the cellar and show me how to change a barrel?'

'Tea's no a problem,' replied Rita, cocking her head in the direction of the kitchen. 'Just get yourself in there and do a mask. However, before I could take you down into the cellar you'll need to take your shoes off. Sure, heels that height...' Both Sally and Rita simultaneously gazed down at Sally's essential stature builders. Rita then slowly continued, '...will end up with you breaking your neck...' *Especially if I give you a good shove*, she thought. '...when you career down the rickety steps.'

Without replying, Sally walked behind the bar, where she reluctantly fished in her bag and brought out a pair of flat-soled plimsoles.

Once she had exchanged her footwear, she was disconcerted by Rita's cackle. 'What's so funny?' Sally asked.

'Just that with the bar being so high and you being so wee all the customers will see is your heid.'

Twenty minutes later, Sally led a disgruntled Rita out of the cellar. 'You sure you've never changed a barrel before?' Rita hissed through clenched teeth.

'No,' was Sally's jubilant response. She should of course have confessed that Ginny had foreseen that Rita would be obstructive rather then willing to teach Sally the basics in how to run a bar. This being the case, Ginny had taken Sally into one of her other bars, the Royal Stuart in Easter Road, and had spent three nights devoted to Sally's tuition.

Sally's eyes were now sweeping the bar-room. First she noted the original ornate cornices that were in need of a lick of paint, as were the narrow, worn floorboards. The black leaded fireplace, where the coals burned brightly, Sally felt added atmosphere to the room and it should be left as it was, even although the tiled surrounds were chipped in places. Turning to Rita, she asked, 'Know something?'

'No till you tell me,' a piqued Rita responded.

'These booths do nothing for this place.' Sally and Rita both looked over towards the six open-fronted cubicles. Cocking her head from side to side, Sally then suggested, 'So I think we should have them taken down – immediately.'

'Immediately?'

'Yes. Like today. So go and find a joiner.'

'Do you think that's wise?' a wide-eyed Rita gasped.

'Most certainly,' a smug Sally confirmed before going over and peering into the nearest booth. 'Them being away would give the place a sense of space and openness,' she hollered back to Rita.

'You could be right, but I don't think Nancy, her motley pals and their paying clients will be too chuffed.'

'Ah. That is the other matter I have to bring up today.'

Rita eyes widened.

'From now on,' Sally continued, unaware that Rita thought she was a fool to try and change the way the pub, which was a gold-mine, was run, 'everyone who comes into this establishment is to act with propriety – that means they will not pick up men for...' Sally paused, gulped and sighed before adding, '...whatever they pick them up for. And any man arriving here drunk from another pub will be thrown out without being served as much as a nip.'

Rita's response was to throw another two large lumps of coal on the fire, although she thought it wasn't necessary, because things in the Four Marys would soon be red-hot!

Disgruntled Josie, who seemed reluctant to alight from the taxi cab, was given a gentle push by Flora, who then fished in her bag for a ten-shilling note to pay the taxi driver, who had turned around to face the women. 'Here,' she said, pushing the money towards the man, 'and I'll give you a wee tip if you'll help us get these cases and boxes into the house.'

The driver glanced into the gloomy court-yard where Flora had indicated the house was. 'No, luv,' he drawled, 'I'm particular where I go. And if my wife found out I had gone into that close I would end up singing soprano.' He now scrutinised Josie and Flora. They certainly weren't the usual Leith fallen women whose faces and bodies were prematurely aged by their dubious trade and too much alcohol. *I wonder*, he thought, *what's brought them down to this hovel?* Getting out of his cab, he came round and hauled two over-laden suitcases and three badly packed boxes from the taxi and dumped them on the pavement before dropping Flora's change into her outstretched hand. 'That's as far as I'm prepared to help you,' he said, 'so let's be having the wee tip you promised me.'

Before she answered, Flora looked down at all of Josie's earthly belongings. They looked just like how Josie herself felt right now – alone and abandoned. 'Tip?' she eventually spat. 'Aye, you certainly could do with one, and here's mine to you: hold on to that wife of yours because the women about here are very choosy about whose money they take for a service.'

By now Josie had picked up the over-packed suitcases and begun walking towards the dark, eerie vennel. Looking down at the three cumbersome boxes, Flora huffed before lugging them up into her arms.

Flora had just started to climb the stairs when she heard a scampering and then a shriek that sent her blood curdling. Throwing the boxes down, she bounded up the rest of the stairs in three leaps. Once inside Josie's flat, she saw that the unshaded electric light bulb was swaying backwards and forwards, casting shadows around the room.

Her attention then rested on Josie, who was perched on the bunker, and it looked to Flora as if she was trying to open the window to jump out. 'What's going on, lassie?' exclaimed Flora, but her voice trailed off when she saw that Josie was not alone in the room. Two rats, fighting on the table over a scrap of food, had joined her.

Without uttering another word, Flora

grabbed a baseball bat, which had obviously been used by the previous occupants to deter the rats, and she began swiping at the vermin until she had them running towards the open door. Once the rats had scampered over the threshold she kicked the door shut, gave a quick prayer of thanks to whoever had left the baseball bat, and then she sank down on a chair.

'Oh Flora,' Josie lamented. 'How can you still say that Sally has done all she can for us when she has no room in her life for you now and she's put me in this rat hole?'

Offering a hand to assist Josie down, Flora replied quietly, 'She's had a hard time. Wish I could have put everything right for her because I owe her.'

Josie huffed again.

'The best daughter any mother ever had, she is.' Flora continued, ignoring Josie's sarcasm. 'And I know she's just gutted that she's only able to look after her own bairns right now.'

Josie's answer to that was another 'huh'.

'Well, you can "huh" all you like, but the truth of it is she's been good to us – both of us. And Josie, in no time at all you'll realise that you have to, and can, stand on your own two feet. And know something else, Josie, a husband and a couple of bairns pulling at your skirts are what you need.'

Josie knew she should respond to Flora,

but memories were now flooding in on her. A husband – she'd nearly had one, and she just knew he would have been a good one, but that blooming stupid war had taken him from her. And without really thinking it through she had given away the most precious thing she had ever had – her daughter. She didn't mean to start sobbing, but she thought just how much better her life would be right now if she was sharing it with... 'Damn and blast,' she shouted before thinking, *Why didn't I give her a name?*

Oblivious to Josie's daydreaming, Flora continued, 'And Sally did say she would make room for me when she gets into her flat at 68 Great Junction Street next week. But – och, Josie. I'm just too old now to be anything but a burden to her and it was me who decided that I should go back to my own wee croft house in Culloden.'

An uneasy silence fell between the two women that was only broken when Flora said, 'Look, Josie, if you think you cannae thole the rats, and remember they'll only come into the house when the tide goes out, or get the enthusiasm... Flora looked about the room, '...to get the rat-catchers in and do the place up ... how about coming to bide with me in Culloden? There's plenty of room there. Could give you a room all to yourself, and the window looks straight over the Moray Firth.'

131

Flora's offer hit Josie like a bomb. She knew she would have to answer Flora and she would have to be diplomatic. So she took her time and analysed every word before she uttered it, which was unlike herself. 'Flora,' she began, going over and taking Flora's hand in hers, 'I'm going to tell you a secret.' Josie eyes roamed around the room as if to make sure there were no inquisitive rats about. 'Now,' she continued, 'this has to be kept between us. You see, it will come as a real surprise to Sally, but our Daisy is on her way over from Australia.'

'Are you saying your half-sister Daisy in coming back home?'

Josie nodded.

'Ah well, I never said, but I thought that when Paddy took her and Luke away to the other end of the earth, I ... well ... your Daisy and Luke were brought up in Iona Street and right enough it might be classed as Edinburgh but you can hardly describe it as the outback.'

Josie pondered as she tried to work out exactly what Flora was saying, but as an answer evaded her, she said, 'And Flora, believe me, I am so grateful for your offer, but I have to be here to welcome Daisy and Luke home.'

'Suppose you're right, but is it not an awful gamble you'll be taking? They are your kith and kin, but – you hardly know them.'

Now it was Josie's time to contemplate and Flora was surprised when she said, 'Look. I know what you're saying – so believe me when I say that if things don't work out with Daisy and Luke when they arrive I'll be on the first train to Inverness.' Josie became pensive again before confiding, 'But I'm a city lassie and the isolation of... Besides that I have to be close to that bitch of a sister of mine. Oh aye, Sally thinks she'll manage without me, but she won't. Never has.'

It was difficult for Flora to hide her laughter. Of course Sally was right in taking the opportunity to get Josie to be responsible for herself, but it was also right that Josie knew Sally was close at hand to support her – and if necessary get her out of the holes she continually dug for herself – not the other way around. Looking at Josie again and recalling her awful history, Flora conceded Sally was a necessity that Josie could never survive without.

When the bar door banged off the wall and the woman catapulted herself in she thought there was no one behind the bar. That was until Sally, who had bent over to massage her aching calves, appeared.

'What can I get you?' Sally enquired politely.

Jerking her thumb and looking to where the cubicles used to be, big Nancy replied in a voice that came from the soles of her boots, 'The stupid idiot who had my workplace, better known as a Nancy's cubbyhole, knocked down.'

Sally knew this was crunch time. She either stood her ground with this woman who was built like an Amazon or she shut up shop. Oh yes, Sally accepted she was dwarfed by Nancy, who in her bare feet stood a good eight inches taller than her. She also noted that Nancy's shoulders were as broad as a wrestler's, and it didn't take much imagination to think that if ever Atlas required a rest from carrying the world on his back then Nancy would be more than able to stand in for him. The only things Sally could see about Nancy that marked her as feminine were her long blonde hair, which was swept up over her head and kept in place by four well-polished tortoiseshell hair combs, her sparkling green eyes and her Madonna-like face.

Stepping up onto an upturned lemonade box, Sally said, 'The person you're looking for is me. And believe me – in no way am I a stupid idiot.'

'That right?' Nancy answered, leaning further over the bar, which caused Sally to fall back but not far enough to tumble off the box.

'It is,' Sally retaliated loudly. 'And please note ... are you a Miss or Mrs?'

Nancy cackled before responding, 'I've missed nothing. And when you get out of hospital you would be doing yourself a favour to remember to call me Mrs Greenfield.'

Sally gulped. Her knees buckled. But she drew herself up and pointing to a recently hung notice on the wall she said, 'Like it says there. From today, and that means right now, with the approval of the Leith Police, there will be no more soliciting in this saloon bar and the management will not serve anyone they consider to be inebriated.'

Nancy laughed. She removed the offending notice from the wall and flung it out of the now open door.

'Atta girl, Nancy, you tell her the story o' the three bears. And while you're at it explain that we rule in here – no her or the thieving bloody brewers and if they dinnae like it they can sling their hooks,' the slurred voice of Sam Steele, who had come into the bar with another six worthies, spat.

'Now, sir, I don't know who you are and what you think you're going to get away with, but let me tell you ... you had better go back to the bar that allowed you to get into the state you're in because you'll not be served here tonight or in the future unless you are sober.'

Raucous laughter echoed around the now very busy pub. Nancy, taking her cue from Sam, got behind the bar and began pulling pints. 'Drinks on the house, boys, because Little Red Riding Hood is in charge and she's incapable of blowing out a candle never mind barring all of us.'

Sally knew flight would be the end of her bar career, so she decided now was the time to fight. She had thought it might come to something like this and so she had planked a walking stick behind the bar. All Nancy knew was a painful whack on the back of her hand that caused her to stop pulling pints, and she whined in pain. She knew immediately that it was Sally who had struck her and, painful as it was, with both hands she grabbed Sally's hair and pulled her out of the bar and into the saloon. 'Stupid bitch,' she hissed, 'so you think you can do me. Well, you'll need an army to help you and where will you get that?'

Flora and Josie had just entered into the salon when they became aware that Sally was in trouble. Without a word being spoken, Josie gave a totally unexpected thump to Nancy's back. However, before she could deliver a second blow, Nancy, who was badly winded, started to buckle at the knees before landing on her back on the floor. Looking up through dazed eyes for her assailant, she was dumbfounded to be confronted with a jubilant Josie, who was being egged on by a sniggering Flora. 'Where will she get an army?' Josie rasped before leaning over Nancy's face.

'Sure she doesnae need one when she has ... us!'

This threat didn't have the desired effect on Nancy, who was lying on the floor like a stranded whale. All she could do was laugh uproariously because of the absurdity of the situation. Here was an old pensioner who looked like a refugee from the poorhouse and a woman who looked as if she had been cut off at the knees trying to put the fear of death into her – her, who could floor a navvy with one hand while throttling a cheating upstart with the other.

Sensing that Nancy wasn't intimidated in any way by either Flora or herself, Josie screamed, 'And if you're thinking we wouldn't have the bottle to sort you out then think again... Or better still go down to Bernard Street and look at the other rats who tried to scare us... You'll easy ken them – they're the ones nursing their fractured skulls.'

Flora's jaw dropped. This was a Josie she'd never seen before. It wasn't that she had thumped Nancy that was surprising, it was the way she had taken the story of the rats and used it to have everybody believe the vermin had been two big strapping men. Nodding, Flora reluctantly conceded that the rat story was just another flight of fancy for Josie, who by the morning would have convinced herself she had sorted out two burly bullies.

Surveying the mayhem about her and being buoyed up by the arrival and actions of Flora and Josie, Sally sprang up on her box again. Eyeing each of the voyeurs in turn and beckoning them to come closer, she smiled sweetly before suggesting, 'Now if anybody else fancies their chances against us, come right up here now!'

With all that was going on, nobody had noticed that the inspector and sergeant from 'D' division headquarters had sauntered in until the obese, ruddy-complexioned sergeant, whose face resembled that of a well-slapped backside, banged his truncheon on the bar. 'Hello, hello,' was his opening remark before warning, 'this here establishment's, or to be truthful this den of iniquity's, licence is up for renewal in three weeks.' He strolled over and pinned up the notice that he had retrieved from the gutter back up on the wall. Menacingly pointing again with his truncheon to the assembly, he went on, 'So these now, let us say, "liberal" rules that *should* have been applied in here will from now on be *strictly adhered to!*'

Nancy was now upright again, and she sauntered saucily over to the sergeant before whispering so loudly that everyone could hear, 'And another condition that has been ignored by *some*, but from tonight will also be strictly adhered to, is that anybody who wishes to purchase from my store will require, whether they are in *uniform or not,* to put his money...' she paused to pat her bosom, '...here on the counter first.'

It was obvious the inspector was aware of, and obviously embarrassed by, his sergeant's dalliances. 'Point taken, Nancy,' was all he said, but the look he gave his sergeant spoke volumes. 'Now, Sergeant Lawson, the other pubs we have to check tonight are the Pale Horse in Henderson Street and the Vine in North Junction Street, so I'll finish up in here and you go to the Pale Horse now and we'll rendezvous...' the Inspector checked his watch before adding, '...in exactly one hour's time at the Vine.'

The disgruntled sergeant grasped immediately that he was being put down. He wasn't surprised, as it was common knowledge within the force that he and David Stock hated each other. Lawson also knew that Stock, who thought he was a disgraceful officer, would like to see him dismissed from the force.

On leaving the premises, Sergeant Lawson thought some more about bloody Inspector Stock, who had blighted his career and held up his advancement. He had concluded long ago that he being a man's man – a bloke who liked a drink, his football, a wee flutter on the gee-gees and bit of hanky-panky on the side – was the real reason why

Bible-punching Stock didn't rate him. But what red-blooded man would want to be like sober, stolid Stock, who went straight home at the end of every shift to look after his invalid wife? Lawson shook his head, thinking, *Is it not enough that the poor lassie has to be saddled with a miserable, joyless nonentity like her husband without also being landed with multiple sclerosis?*

As soon as Lawson departed, David Stock removed his hat and laid it on the bar. 'Now, who is in charge here when Ginny's away?'

Getting down off her box, Sally came around to the front of the bar and extended her hand to David. 'My name is Sally Stuart, and once Ginny has me trained up I'll be in charge here.'

'That so?'

Sally nodded in unison with Flora and Josie.

'And...' David continued, turning to Flora and Josie.

'Flora here is my mother-in-law, who I am trying to persuade to stay here in Leith, but she is adamant that she'll be on the Inverness train next Monday morning.'

'And I certainly will be. You see, Inspector, I used to only be Mrs Mop around here, but when I found out...' Flora turned to Sally and winked mischievously, '...my daughter-in-law was going to be my boss, I stacked my pail behind that door and I'm now head-ing for my own wee croft, where *I'll* be in charge. And Josie here is Sally's sister and she's going to be staying in one of the flats behind the King's Wark.'

'You never are,' David gasped. 'Hasn't anybody told you that it's rat-infested?'

'They didn't, but Flora and I found out for ourselves tonight. That's why we're here to talk to Sally.'

Accepting that he was an intruder in this family get-together, David pursed his lips, lifted his hat up and donned it. 'I mustn't keep you any longer. Just want to say you can rely on the local police to give you every assistance that you require to get things sorted out here. Oh, by the way, Sergeant Lawson is being moved inside to be a desk sergeant and a Sergeant Green will be taking over this patch.'

Before leaving, he nodded to each of the women in turn, even Nancy, who was still hanging about.

'See him,' Nancy said when David was out of earshot, 'now he is a man that not only would I not take money from for a service but I would pay him for doing me the favour!'

Sally didn't know how to answer Nancy. It was true the inspector was a good-looking man who carried his mature years well. She did think he had a lot going for him and not only because he had an honest face and a way of making people think that they mattered. There was something else about him... *Why, she wondered, do I feel myself getting hot and embarrassed when I'm thinking about him? Have I not had enough of men to keep me going the rest of my life? Besides, he is a happily married man.* Noticing everybody was now staring at her, she suddenly blurted, 'Look, Nancy, you now know you cannot pick up men in here...'

'Aye, but mostly it's the men who pick me up, so would that still be okay?'

Exasperated, Sally shook her head. Nancy got the message. Sally then gave a small compromise. Lifting a cloth to wipe the bar, she looked Nancy straight in the eye before saying, 'But you could still have a drink and because of the night we've had...'

'On the house?'

Sally nodded.

'In that case make it a double gin and tonic with ice and a slice of lemon to finish it off. Oh, and by the way, Sally, what's more important to me is ... can I still have the use of your lavvy? See that one they call the ladies in the Standard Bar? Sure, no self-respecting woman would put a foot in it, never mind her behind on the seat.'

Closing time couldn't come quick enough for the three women. As soon as the door was shut, Flora collected all the glasses and

142

began to wash them. Josie, who had been astonished at the amount of money that had crossed the bar, started to cash up.

'Here, Sally,' Josie shouted. 'How much do I leave in the till as a float?'

Sally's mind was still going over the happenings of the last three hours, which caused her to wonder if she would ever make a success of running a bar – especially a bar in Leith that had been notorious and was known correctly as the Jungle. And now she had the unenviable task of making it into a 'must' place to go. She looked up and said, 'Never you mind the float right now, Josie. Both you and Flora come over here until you tell me about the rats that tried to assault you.'

Once they were seated around the table, Flora began, 'Look, Sally, did you ever visit that place you thought was suitable for Josie?'

Sally shook her head.

'Then let me tell you the place is overrun with rats, real rats. Two of them were in the flat – welcoming committee I think they were – chased them out the door, I did.'

Gulping and shaking, Sally placed a trembling hand over Josie's. 'I didn't know. Ginny said all the houses in that pend were being renovated just as soon as they could get the squatting tenants out.'

'Squatting tenants out? They'll need ten squads of rat-catchers to tackle the vermin and the auld siege of Leith will have nothing on the struggle they'll have to get the human squatters out.'

Still covering Josie's hand with hers and looking straight into her eyes, Sally mumbled, 'I'm so sorry. I thought it was a place you could be on your own – become responsible for yourself.' Sally turned to Flora. 'Flora, you know I don't want you to go to Culloden. I'd like you to stay here with me, Helen and Bobby – we need you. I can't remember life without you and the children have only known a life where you were part of it.'

'Sally, I'm old. I'm gutted, and I hope your son never roasts your heart like Harry has blistered mine.' Sally tried to interrupt, but Flora silenced her with a wave of her hand. 'No, hear me out. It's my wish to go home now, back to my roots, and what I haven't told you is that my sister Shonag needs me to be close at hand.'

Sally, who was feeling guilty at being so wrapped up in her own problems that she hadn't noticed that Flora had more on her mind than Harry and herself breaking up, tried to get Flora to look at her, but Flora's eyes were downcast. 'Why didn't you say? What's wrong with Shonag? Is William alright?'

Leaning her arms on the table so she could cup her chin in her hands, Flora began, 'It's

William that's the problem. Broken-hearted, Shonag is. And before you ask, I don't know the full story. Another of his love affairs gone wrong. What I do know is, she needs me, so I require to go back home where both us were bairns the-gether ... and both of us have problem sons who need sorting out.'

Sally allowed time to tick by before she said, 'Fine, Flora, I can live with that, but please remember that if ever you want to come back – I'll make room for you. After all, I'll never forget that it was you who made room for me ... and my brother Peter when we needed it.'

Both women nodded to each other before Sally turned to Josie. 'Now to you. Until the powers that be get that flat of yours habit-able, you just move into 68 Great Junction Street with us next week. And before you say anything, I can't give you a bed to yourself, never mind a room. Sharing a bed-settee with me is what you'll have to settle for. So make sure your keep your toenails short.'

By the time Sally arrived back at Elgin Ter-race, Flora and Josie were already there. They had come home by taxi after picking up Josie's belongings from the Bernard Street flat.

'Fancy a cuppa, Sally?'

'Thanks, Flora. All night I've been sur-rounded by drink and as I'm strictly teetotal

I never...' Before Sally could go on, the doorbell sounded.

The three women looked from one to the other. 'Helen and Bobby in bed?'

Flora nodded. 'Just like you asked, I checked on them when I came in.'

'Then who can it be at this time of night?'

The insistent ringing of the bell started again and the trio dashed up the hallway to open the door.

'Hello. Know you're not expecting us until tomorrow, but we managed to get on the late train this afternoon. Oh. By the way, Sally, could you pay the taxi? We're out of change.'

'Well, blow me, if it's not our young Daisy. My, how you've grown, and Luke, you must be all of six feet and as handsome as Clark Gable,' exclaimed Flora. 'Come away in both of you. Can you manage to scrape up the money to pay the cab man, Sally?'

'Aye, after I've scraped myself up off the floor.' Turning to Josie, who was trying to melt into the wall, Sally asked through gritted teeth, 'What did she mean when she said that I wasn't expecting them until to-morrow?'

Josie waited until Sally, having paid, off the taxi driver, closed the door before she pleaded, 'Look, it's not my fault. You see, Margo sent them an invitation to her wedding. And that was only natural, as Daisy

146

and Luke are our kinfolk.'

'And I take it she also asked Paddy and he'll be expecting me to stump up a taxi fare for him tomorrow?'

'No! The reason Daisy and Luke never made Margo's wedding...'

'Is our Margo arranged it in such a hurry they couldn't have got here in time – unless they'd come by broomstick.'

'Right enough, Sally, they would've liked to have flown but with air fares ... well, you need to save up for ten years with Magnus the travel agent round the corner to be able to afford them.'

Disgruntled, Sally started to walk towards the living room, but Josie hauled her back by grabbing her arm. 'Even if Margo had,' she whispered, 'given them plenty of notice, they couldn't have been here for her big do because...' Josie paused, wrung her hands and inhaled before adding, '...you see, Sally, our Daisy was being a bridesmaid at...' She hesitated again. 'Now before I tell you, promise you'll no holler and laugh?'

Sally shook her head and then nodded.

'Paddy's wedding.'

'Are you saying some other woman has been stupid enough...' Sally chuckled loudly, causing Josie to put her hand over Sally's mouth.

'Yeah. But don't say anything. Luke's peeved about it.'

When Sally and Josie eventually joined the others, Daisy was the first to speak. 'Look, when I wrote and told Margo and Josie we would be coming home I didn't know...' She stopped to glance at the far wall, where all the packing cases were stacked, '...that you were on the move.'

'No need to concern, yourself,' Sally quickly assured her. 'Somehow we'll find you a bed.'

'But why are you flitting?'

It had been a long, difficult and tiring day, and the last thing Sally wished to do was to admit that Harry had deserted her, especially to Luke, who still had the habit of unnerving her. 'I'll let Josie explain the whole shameful story to you whilst I get on with making you some tea. When did you last eat?'

'Early this afternoon, you see we're stony...'

'Luke, we are not penniless yet. We have ... how much was it when we last counted it?'

'Nine shillings and sixpence.'

The noise of Sally filling the kettle fortunately hid the sound of the wearisome sighs and groans that escaped her.

It took quite a bit of juggling before Sally had managed to get everyone a place to sleep. The wee small hours of the morning had crept up on her before she found herself with time to think about all that had happened.

When everybody was abed, Sally sat down to ponder. It wasn't just Daisy and Luke arriving and expecting to be housed that niggled. It was finding out that Paddy had got himself hitched to a lassie just four years older than his twenty-one-year-old daughter, Daisy. And okay, his bride was an Aborigine and if he was to be believed native Australians matured more quickly, but surely the young lassie wouldn't want an old man... Sally shivered and grimaced. Scratching her head, she then thought back to Daisy saying that what she loved most about Australia was the weather. She beamed from ear to ear when she had continued, 'Know something, Sally, if you decided that in a week's time you would have a picnic on the beach then you could be assured the sun would be shining that day.'

'Not like here,' Sally mused. 'Aye, here you have to be quick and the minute the sun puts in an appearance you have to dash down to Portobello and fight for a space on the sand.'

Daisy had become dreamlike when she related what she had missed the most while she had been away in Australia. Naturally, what had brought her back to Scotland was the missing of family and friends and the longing to meander on the weel-kent streets. To Sally's surprise, Daisy tearfully stuttered that she also missed her mother so very much. But then she had lived so different a life from Sally. True, they had the same mother, but in the twenty years that separated them Peggy had become a different person, possibly because she had married Paddy, Daisy's father. No way would he have tolerated anyone mistreating his children.

Reluctantly, Sally had to address what the coming back of Luke would mean for her. Tonight as they ate warm buttered toast and drank cup after cup of tea he confessed he had come back because the reason he had gone to Australia was that he had promised himself that one day he would exact revenge on his father for having hastened his mother's departure. Engaging Sally with a hostile stare, he went on, 'But on Dad's stag night he took me aside and told me a story ... and now I know for certain my *father*, even although she begged him to put an end to her suffering, did *not* help my mother away.'

Sally, quaking inside, was not sure where Luke's suppositions were going. Evidently, where his mother was concerned he still had scores to settle. Was he saying, albeit surreptitiously, that revenge for her lay here in Scotland? Luke, still smiling at Sally with a smile that never reached his cold eyes, then went on to say that he was satisfied, very satisfied, to know that there was a God and that at this present moment he had no need to wreak vengeance.

His second, more disconcerting, bomb-shell was that he intended to stay in Edinburgh and apply to join the Edinburgh City Police. She knew he would probably be accepted, because he was more than above the regulation height and had all the other necessary qualifications.

The following morning, the most pressing matter of the day for Sally was where Daisy and Luke could be housed once she and her children had to vacate spacious, elegant Elgin Terrace.

Deliberating on the situation, Sally thought that Daisy wouldn't be a problem, as she could bunk in with Helen. But Luke, well, there just wouldn't be room for him when they moved into Great Junction Street. It wasn't, she lied to herself, that she didn't wish to have Luke in the same house as herself. But well... She paused in her contemplations and blushed before admitting she would use the reason that fourteen-year-old Bobby had a leg problem, which meant he not only had to have a bed to himself but also a room.

So what could she do about Luke? A sly smile crossed her face when she recalled that she was going to seek out the old Leith rat-catcher's son. Now she knew the rat-catcher had died a long time ago and that his son, who had carried on in his father's footsteps, would now be nearing retirement age, but she was sure he still lived in or near Bowling Green Street. So she would take a wee detour on her way to the Four Marys and seek him out.

As luck would have it, finding the rat-catcher was easy. He still lived in the house where he had been born. What was even better was that he said that by visiting the flat in Bernard Street regularly he would be able to keep the vermin under control.

Sally waited until she got home from work at night before she said, 'You'll never know who came into the pub today.'

'Dad,' exclaimed Bobby.

This answer back-footed Sally. 'No. A rat-catcher.'

'Hope you told them where Maggie lives.'

'No, Bobby,' Sally, who was the only person not laughing, replied. 'I didn't, because he only puts an end to four-legged rats.'

Looking around the room, Luke asked, 'But why do you need a rat-catcher?'

Sally laughed, 'Of course with all that went on last night we didn't tell you that I had got a flat for Josie, but the sitting tenants – two *very* small rats – frightened her. That's why she's coming to live with me in Great Junction Street.' She appeared to grow pensive. 'Imagine her wishing to crush in at Great Junction Street when she could have a wee flat all to herself once the rats are evicted. More tea or toast anyone?'

As luck would have it, Luke rose to the bait. Turning on his charm, which had captivated everybody but Sally, he smiled before saying, 'Look, Sally, if the rat-catcher can get the pests out, I would be happy to move in.'

Sally put up her hand in protest; however, before she could beg him not to think about moving in there, Daisy interrupted, 'And as we have never lived apart, I will go with you, Luke.'

This was not what Sally wished to hear. Luke going there to live with rats she was happy, very happy, about, but sweet Daisy, she... 'No, you couldn't,' she quickly blurted. 'You see it only has a cold-water tap, no bathing facilities and an outside lavatory.'

Both Daisy and Luke shrieked and giggled.

'What's so funny?' demanded Sally.

'Just that in the last five years or so,' Luke said, winking to Daisy.

'On and off,' she added, patting him on the shoulder.

'We've lived,' continued Luke, 'wild in the outback and back streets, and seen those Australian rats, monsters they are, but when they heard we were moving in we didn't need to evict them.'

'You're right there, Luke,' Daisy managed to splutter through her laughter. 'They committed hara-kiri by jumping out the window – without opening it.'

Waverley Station is a place of joy and sadness. Today as Sally stood on the draughty platform she felt as if her right arm was being hauled from its socket. Could it be only four weeks since the family's life had been turned upside down? A month ago they were a family unit that was the envy of all their friends and neighbours. Then Harry left them and the real reason he had taken that shattering step was still evading Sally. And now Flora was taking the early morning train to Inverness. No longer would she be part of their everyday lives. No longer would she be Sally's rock to cling to.

Just before the guard blew his whistle for the train to depart, Flora asked Margo, 'Why are you always looking down the platform? Are you expecting someone?'

'J-j-j-j-just my Johnny,' Margo stuttered before waving to the man and woman running up towards them.

'Good grief,' Flora shouted before quickly hugging Bobby, Helen and then Sally. 'Quick, I must get aboard before they reach here.'

'But Granny,' protested Margo, 'He's your son and she's...'s

'The whore that has broken my heart,' Flora replied, as she jumped aboard the train and banged the door shut.

'Mum, Mum, please wait, I have to speak to you,' Harry pleaded. 'You've always got on with Maggie and she wants just to be friends with you.'

Flora lowered the door window. 'I'll speak to you again when you've come to your senses and begged Sally's forgiveness. And as to be being friends with your bidie-in, let me tell you, it was Sally that gave her houseroom. As far as I'm concerned she's a whoring *Jezebel* and I wouldn't spit on her if she was...'

Whatever else Flora said nobody would ever know, as it was drowned out by the guard using his whistle to signal the train to leave.

Sally, Helen and Bobby waved and waved until the train was out of sight. Turning, they noticed, but were not surprised, that Harry, Maggie and Margo had scuttled away.

4

1964
'Sally,' Rita called out from the kitchen of the Four Marys bar, 'what are we going to call the soup of the day today?'

'What's in it?' was Sally's uninterested reply.

'Anything that was lying about,' was Rita's exasperated retort. 'But I don't think you'll sell many plates of it if you call it "anything-that-was-lying-aboot soup".'

It had taken three years for the two women to reach this state of camaraderie. Both now not only respected each other but also valued each other's talents.

Sally remembered vividly how vociferous Rita had been when she had floated the idea of providing wholesome lunches. 'This is a Leith pub,' Rita had exclaimed. 'We're no the Wee Windaes in Edinburgh, where they kid themselves on that they are a restaurant and serve your chips up in a basket.'

Nonetheless, Sally had persisted in the change from providing women to sex-hungry men to supplying nourishing meals to peckish workers.

So successful was the change that now the Four Marys was known as a place of respect-ability at lunchtimes. In the evening they still had more than a few males seeking solace in the Jungle, but Sally, after refusing to serve them any alcohol, very nicely sent them in the direction of the Henderson Street and Broad Pavement hostelries.

The other advantage of Rita finding out that she was a first-class plain cook was that her confidence was boosted. So much so that when Sally asked her last week if she thought she could run things on her own for five days whilst she went up to visit Flora, she had jumped at the chance.

Now Sally herself had learned quite a lot about the bar trade in the last three years. For instance, she knew that when she left Rita in charge she wouldn't do anything to damage the good stock-taking record. She would, of course, have a wee fiddle that Sally could live with – like bringing in a bottle each of whisky and gin and then selling them over the counter by the nip and thus making a healthy profit for herself. This practice was widespread and normal in the trade.

Rita, chalk in hand, was now standing at the blackboard. 'How about I call it Granny's Broth? 'Cause that's how aw grannies made their soup. Just threw in anything they could lay their hands on.'

Sally nodded.

'Here, Sally, you've been awfy quiet since you got back from Culloden. Did you fight another battle or something up there?'

'Culloden is no the problem. It's... Och, Rita, it's this blooming wedding that's getting my goat Imagine it. The divorce is just through and there is philandering Harry rushing to get hitched again, in a kilt no less and with a piper blowing him into the registry office along with a bimbo he's got himself in tow with now.'

'Could be worse,' a pensive Rita drawled whilst placing two steaming mugs of tea on the table. 'Ever thought, you could be your auld pal, Maggie? Aye, imagine how you'd feel if you'd scunnered aw your true pals and now your dream man had dumped you for a younger, bonnier model the minute he was free to get hitched again.' Rita, sitting herself down in front of Sally, paused, lit up a cigarette, blew the smoke upwards and sucked in her cheeks before delivering the knockout blow. 'Mind you, I always wondered why your Harry left you for Maggie, but as they say, men never look at the mantelpiece when they're poking the fire.'

Sally completely ignored Rita's remarks. She had more to think about than Maggie. 'I'm really grateful to you for tending the pub whilst I was away. I just had to tell Flora face to face about Harry getting married again, and not to Maggie.' Sally sighed. 'But she already knew because not only had he sent her an invitation but he had also intimated that he and his next missus, Felicity, were going to ask Margo to be Matron of Honour.'

Rita cackled. 'Matron of Honour. Your Margo and Harry wouldnae ken honour if it pitched up and bit them on the bum. By the way, forget them two traitors. That was a great idea of yours to get Josie to fill in behind the bar. Now there's a real bonny face, and is she not wearing well at thirty-five?'

'Aye, but then she's never been shackled to a useless man and been at the beck and call of not only three bairns but a Peter Pan sister as well.'

'Gie credit where it's due, Sally. Josie did well at being the mein host behind the bar when you were away. And she was promoting nothing but beer.'

Sally huffed.

'Okay,' continued Rita. 'She did have more than a few propositions, but she never...'

'Aye, I'll bet she did.'

Rita shrugged and changed the subject by saying, 'Know something, Sally, there's an awfy sadness about Josie at times. Think that's why your brother always waits for her after he's finished his shift. And here, do you ken he's probably going to get a bravery award?'

The mention of Luke still had an adverse effect on Sally. It was just her luck that after he had done his training at the Scottish Police College he'd been attached to Edinburgh 'D' Division, whose headquarters were in Charlotte Street. And if all that was not enough to annoy Sally, hadn't he been on the Shore beat for six months now.

'Are you listening to me, Sally?'

'No, it's eleven o'clock and I'm opening up. And here, I hope that's your cigarette that I smell burning...' she sniffed before going on, '...and not the pot of anything that's lying-about soup.'

Friday nights in Leith were always busy for the police. Last Friday had been even more so. Thirty-year-old good-looking bachelor Luke, who was everybody's darling but Sally's, was doing the back shift – two in the afternoon until ten at night.

He'd just hung up his civvies jacket when the morning constable, John Thomson, looked quizzically at it before saying, 'Suppose that means you and your pal, Rab, in "B" division, are going for a few pints and a birl around the dance floor when you're finished.'

'Sure are,' replied Luke, doing a soft-shoe shuffle. 'And who the lucky lassie that will land me tonight is, I do not know.'

'Know something, you're like your sister Josie; you're going to leave it too late to get hitched like me...'

'With two out-of-control teenagers thrown in.'

'Aye, and they would help you qualify for a police house in Clermiston and kiss goodbye to that houff...'

'John, that "houff", as you put it, is a well-furnished and -maintained home for not only me and McAllister, my half-wild cat that sees to it that no vermin lives longer than a minute if it is daft enough to invade our home, but also my sister Daisy, who bides there when she's on leave from the hospital.'

'Aye, somebody told me that your sister Sally had brought down two feral kittens from Inverness way and that they were both great hunters.'

'They are. One she gave to me, McAllister, named after the man who gave her them, and the other one, Sheba, she kept herself to keep the Four Marys rat-free too.'

Quickly forgetting the cats, John surprised and annoyed Luke when he lustfully mumbled, 'Here, and talking about your sister Daisy, see the next time I need treatment at Leith Hospital I hope it'll be your Daisy, Daisy, give me your answer do who will be applying the plasters.'

Exasperated, Luke mumbled, 'Look, just get ringing into headquarters and let them know that you're going off duty and I'm taking over.'

Within ten minutes of John leaving, Luke was out, where he loved to be, on the beat. One of his first ports of call, which he had to do before 3 p.m. closing time, was the Four Marys. He just reached the door when Sam Steele staggered out. 'Oh, not you again,' Luke exclaimed, dodging out of Sam's way. 'It's only two o'clock in the day and by the looks of you I should run you in.'

'Look, son,' Sam lisped, 'that bitch in there...'

'My sister Josie...'

161

'Are you saying the bitch is your sister? Well, no offence meant. But she's a right Bible-punching git. No sell me ony mair drink, she'll no.' Luke remained silent. Sam went on, 'So I'll meander ower to the the Ship Inn – and do you ken when you ask for a nip and a pint in there that's what you get with naebudy trying to get you to change your mind and hae a plate o' soup or mince and tatties instead.'

Sam spat on the ground. Disgusted, Luke stuck out his foot, which Sam tripped on before staggering out into the roadway. 'Mind how you go, Sam,' Luke hollered after him. 'You could end up in the water, and see if you get any drunker and I see you stagger into the drink I'll no jump in to save you.'

Before Luke entered the pub, he heard Sam starting to recite 'Tam o' Shanter'. It reminded Luke that Sam was an educated man who had fallen on hard times. The second line, 'And drouthy neibors, neibors meet,' was still ringing in Luke's ears when he stepped inside to be warmly greeted by Josie.

Lifting a pint glass, Josie asked, 'Need refreshment, Luke?'

Luke shook his head. 'No. Never drink until I'm about to go off duty.'

'Aye, but you never refuse a plate of warming soup,' Rita replied, dishing him up the delicacy.

During his shift, Luke dealt with drunks, shoplifters, lost children and two domestics, one of which was a husband beaten up by his wife, although he withdrew the charges against her before Luke had finished writing up the complaint – but then it was Leith, and what man would admit to being a battered husband?

Busy as he was, though, he managed to rendezvous with his opposite number in 'B' division, where Granton trawlers still docked on Fridays, and pick up a pauckle of fish that he would hand into the Four Marys. The parcel, of course, included delicacies for hard-working McAllister and Sheba.

On his way back from his fish delivery, he noticed a young sailor slumped against the Bernard Street wall of the King's Wark. Apprehensively approaching the weeping man, Luke discovered he was the young Irish sailor whose ship had been in dry dock for a few weeks three months ago. During the lad's imposed stay in Leith he had got friendly not only with Luke but also with one of the obliging ladies. So infatuated had he become with Marie that he had got her to promise to give up working on the streets, and when she agreed to do so he left her a weekly settlement that she collected at the shipping agents.

Kneeling down beside the man, Luke asked, 'What's up, Irish?'

163

Between sobs, snuffles and pauses, the man managed to mutter, 'Said I would be her only love and left her money to keep her going straight and ... I arrived here on an early tide ... and went up to our place ... and not only was she with one man ... but another two were waiting.'

Luke wanted to help the man, whose name he didn't know except that everybody called him Irish, so getting upright and then dragging Irish up beside him he looked over to the dock before saying, 'Look, there are better fish in that dock there than her.'

To his surprise, the man blurted, 'The dock – that's where I'm thinking of throwing myself, or maybe it would be better if I cut her throat.'

Luke, who had lost count of the number of times that people had said they would commit suicide and then decided to solve their problem with more drink, looked at his watch. 'Look, Irish, it's just fifteen minutes until I finish my shift, so as I want to go dancing tonight don't commit suicide or justifiable homicide until the night shift comes on at ten o'clock.'

Irish sniffed. 'Okay. Look, just take me over the road and I'll get another drink while I'm waiting for the night shift to come on.'

Five minutes later, Luke was in the police box that was situated just at the end of the

164

Commercial Bridge. He had finished all his police reports, changed his shoes and taken off his police jacket to don his brand new Jackson the Tailor's blazer when a frantic knocking at the door stopped his merry whistling. Opening the door, he said, 'Okay, George, stop the fooling. You know it's my partying night so just come in and take over.'

'I'm no George,' the boiler-suited middle-aged man blurted. 'I'm here because I think you should ken there's a man in the water needing saved ... and I cannae swim.'

Luke peered out from the box and was horrified to see the man in the middle of the dock screaming for help was none other than Irish. 'Oh, bloody hell,' he shouted whilst racing along the bridge. On arrival at the dock wall, he removed his jacket and shoes and then dived in. On surfacing, he realised he had swallowed a couple of mouthfuls of the stinking water. Before thinking of his own safety he grabbed hold of bobbing, panicking Irish and was dragging him towards the iron steps that were situated at the side of the pier when drunken Sam, who had seen Luke dive in and thinking in his inebriated state that he should rescue him, leapt into the dock too.

By the time Sam surfaced, Luke had begun pushing Irish up the steps but was suddenly hampered when Sam swam over to them and starting dragging Luke and Irish back under

165

the water.

The situation had become so chaotic that none of the three knew who was rescuing who, which resulted in them all being in danger of drowning. Luckily the ever-dependable George had now taken up the night shift and, climbing down the steps, he somehow managed, with the aid of a long pole, to drag all three to safety.

Unfortunately they had now swallowed several mouthfuls of the filthy, polluted, germ-infested water. 'I think I will die of the plague,' Luke gasped before the ambulance arrived.

'Naw, laddie,' answered George. 'It's Yellow River Fever that'll take you away if we din-nae get you to Leith Hospital in the next ten minutes to get your stomach pumped, your body showered and your smart arse used as a pincushion.'

'And what aboot me and Irish?' demanded Sam.

'Och,' replied George, 'the two o' you'll survive. Your main organs are all pickled.' He then laughed uproariously. 'You see, nae self-respecting germ wants to be killed off by stagnant McEwan's Best.'

About three in the morning, Luke, who had been showered, had his stomach pumped and had been injected against all sorts of infectious troubles – even pregnancy he suspected – was ready to leave the hospital.

He was grateful for all the treatment, painful as some of it was, that he had been given in the last few hours. He now knew why the community of Leith loved this old hospital.

Prior to the National Health Service coming into being, Leith Hospital had been built and its upkeep assured by the distinctive community of Leith, who cherished their beloved place. Always they were assured, rich or poor, of getting the help they required there.

While thinking about the hospital and its place in Leith, Luke wondered how many sailors, fishermen, drunks and attempted suicides had had landed in the water and then been revived in the hospital. *It must total thousands in the last two centuries*, he mused.

Daisy, who was four years younger than himself, was a staff nurse in the hospital. She had been a junior nurse here because she was of the opinion that the training and support she would receive would be second to none.

On being wheeled into hospital, he was thankful to discover that Daisy was the senior staff nurse on duty.

She did try to persuade Luke to stay in the hospital until after breakfast time at least. Luke being Luke, he was determined to go, so he demanded of her that she fetch his jacket and shoes. 'What jacket and shoes?'

she enquired.

'My good blazer and dancing shoes,' he spluttered, spitting out some more gunge from his mouth. 'I kicked them off before I jumped in to save these two idiots.' Luke continued looking at Sam and Irish, who were quite happy to stay tucked up in bed until daybreak. 'Sure someone must have picked them up for me.'

'Picked them up? I think they did, but for themselves.'

'But just a minute, I have another three payments before that jacket is truly mine.'

Daisy just shrugged before lifting up a water-sodden empty wallet. 'Now they haven't robbed you of everything. Look...' She now held the disintegrating article in her hand, '...wasn't it nice of them to return your wallet so you could fling it in the bucket yourself!'

Luke just shrugged and, borrowing one of the hospital dressing gowns, he made for the door of the ward.

'Just a minute, Luke. Since you insist on going home at this unearthly hour, I'll show how you can get out without inconveniencing anyone.'

'Oh, good.'

Daisy and Luke arrived at the tunnel that linked the hospital to the nurses' home. However, as it was a dark, damp corridor Luke shivered.

'Are you sure you're alright?' Daisy enquired.

'Aye. Just a bit shaky, so give me your arm.'

They were halfway up the tunnel when Luke stuttered, 'Daisy, I think I should have stayed in bed. You see, I'm now hearing horrible sounds.'

'Like what?'

'A cracking – crunching – scampering.'

'Don't be daft, you're not hearing things – that noise is your size 10s crushing the scuttling cockroaches to death. At night this place is alive with them!'

The most annoying thing for Sally about last Friday's shenanigans was that Luke had been put up for the Royal Humane Society's Bravery Award for saving Irish. She smirked, thinking how he would be in good company when the Duke of Gloucester, no less, carried out the ceremony, because hadn't drunken Sam Steele also been nominated for the award – his was for jumping in to save Luke!

Three days later, one of the last of the lunchtime customers to come into the Four Marys was none other than Nancy. 'What's brought you in here?' Sally asked.

Nancy squinted up at the blackboard that displayed the menu of the day. 'Well, first of all, no your mince and tatties. Cannae abide mince and tatties with nae carrots in it. So I'll just hae the soup.'

'And?'

'And, Sally, as you know it's too early in the day for me to be working so that means I'm here for another reason.'

'Like what?'

Nancy let time pass. She was enjoying keeping Sally's curiosity dangling. Eventually she slowly uttered, 'A business meeting with none other than Dora Noyce's right-hand woman.'

'What? Oh here, she's no thinking of opening up a high-class knocking shop here in Leith, is she?'

'No. But after we've discussed the business she wishes to put forward, I just might get her to give me some pointers on how to draw up a management plan.'

'Management plan?' Sally spluttered through her giggles. 'You just have to be joking.'

'No. Know something? Dora's got it right. There comes a time when you have to admit to yourself that you're past the rough and tumble of the front line and move up into management.'

'That right?'

'Aye, and Dora does it so well. She has fifteen lassies working full-time in the house at Danube Street and when there is more work than they can handle she calls in another five part-timers. And do ye ken they aw hae to sign up to her strict employment conditions?'

'Like what?'

'Ooh. Like, they have to put so much of their earnings away for the days that they're no able to lie down on the job. And if they are caught sharing their earnings with a pimp then they're dismissed immediately on the grounds of gross misconduct.'

Sally, helpless with laughter, began to wonder if she was having a nightmare and concluded that she was when Nancy went on, 'And see, when them up in the High Street decided to try and close Dora doon, she called a press meeting in the North British Hotel, and dressed in her mandatory half-mink jacket with matching hat she slowly drawled, "My clients come from all walks of life, from the top echelons to the bottom of society, and up till now I have always been discreet – very discreet. But you know something, the busiest time of the year for me is when the Church of Scotland General Assembly meet!" Evidently Sally,' Nancy went on, 'the queue's right up the street then.' Nancy, who had enjoyed uttering every word, sniffed and rubbed under her nose with her hand before gleefully continuing, 'And the result of that wee press meeting is – not one single God-praising soul is spouting that she should ever be closed down!'

Before Sally could comment, the door opened and in swept an elegant, statuesque black woman who was also dressed in the mandatory clothing of successful Edinburgh business ladies – a fur jacket with matching jaunty hat and at least six diamond rings glinting on her fingers. 'I'm here to meet...'

Nancy quickly sprung to her feet and offered the lady her hand. 'Me. I'm Nancy, the Ports Madam.' Nancy now turned to Sally. 'Sally, be a pal and change my order to two plates of broth. My friend here will be dining with me.'

Still unable to control her merriment, Sally had to dive into the kitchen.

'Good you've come in. Did I hear right that Nancy wants soup for herself and her pal?' exclaimed Rita.

'Aye.'

'But there's only enough left for one.'

'Don't worry. These ladies have gone so far up in the world they'll no notice that you've doctored the soup by...'

'But how will I do that?' Rita quickly interrupted.

'Just add some water to it – like you do to the whisky when I'm not looking – and also fling in an Oxo cube and they'll think they're consuming consommé,' Sally chirped before going over to the blackboard and rubbing out 'broth' and writing 'consommé'.

Once Nancy's luncheon friend had left,

Sally sidled over to a crestfallen Nancy. 'What's the score then?' she asked, lifting up the empty soup plates.

Nancy sighed. 'It seems that a certain American ship that has been oot for weeks on manoeuvres in the Baltic – trying to put the frighteners up the Russians or something like that – is coming into Leith docks. Teeming with sex-starved sailors it is. So that means the fifteen resident lassies in Danube Street will no be able to cope.'

'Aye, but she has others she can usually call on.'

'So she has. But just like the thing – one of our cod war ships that's been oot for months terrorising the Icelandic fishing fleet has just docked in Liverpool and the lassies are away there. Too good a chance to miss, that is.'

'Oh, so she wants you and some of your pals to help out at Danube Street?'

'No exactly,' huffed Nancy. 'She wants me to ask some of the *young* ones if they would like the chance. Of course, they would need to go to the Family Planning Clinic and have a health check first. But they would be well paid and their grub and bed would be thrown in.'

Sally took a long, hard look at Nancy. *It's strange*, she thought, *that three years ago I would never have considered starting up a friendship with a woman who – well – sold her favours*. Even although she did not allow

173

Nancy to solicit in the Four Marys, she was always pleased to see her and pass the time of day with her. Six months ago their friendship had grown so strong that Sally had the temerity to ask Nancy, who had a complimentary double gin and tonic complete with ice and lemon in front of her, 'How can you do it, Nancy? Some of these men you well...'

Nancy lifted the glass to her mouth and swallowed a good gulp. Then, swilling the glass, she began, 'If it wasn't for good old Gordon's here, I couldn't.' She took another swig. 'To be truthful, Sally, I wish I hadn't started. I was young and...' She rose and looked in the mirror. '...good looking, very good looking. My supposedly loving father told me it was easy money.' She cackled. 'When we lived in Ferrier Street he brought men up from the pub for my sister and me...' Nancy shook her head. 'Only ten and twelve we were, Sally. Just bits o' bairns.'

'You have a sister?'

'Had. You see, my Bertha couldnae cope with life on the streets, or at hame either, so her ... ashes are scattered in Seafield's remembrance gardens. Now do you think she would want to remember?' Nancy sighed before adding, 'Ken something, Sally, sometimes I think I should follow her example because what else is there for me now?'

Before Sally could respond, the door opened and in flounced Ginny. As usual she was dressed in her soft-beige mink jacket and her hands were adorned with several diamond rings.

'Is it not closing time?' Ginny asked, whilst looking at the jewel-encrusted face of her watch.

'Right enough,' Sally agreed, looking up at the clock that she kept ten minutes fast before signalling to Rita to close the door.

Turning her attention to Nancy, Ginny quietly suggested, 'That'll be you off.'

Nancy nodded and proceeded out of the door.

Sally wasn't happy at Nancy being dismissed like that, but Ginny was the licensee and she had been good to her, so it was not in Sally's interest to pick a fight with the hand that had not only fed her but had given her all her responsibilities as well.

'Before you go, Rita, be a sweetheart and make Sally and me a cup of tea. We have a lot to discuss.'

Sally had forgotten it was the end of the month and Ginny always came in around then to have a management update.

Once Rita had departed, Ginny removed her fur jacket and Sally poured up the tea. 'Business is good, Ginny. We are up on last month's takings and there's been no real trouble,' Sally was delighted to report.

'Good,' replied Ginny, lazily stirring her tea. 'Now, Sally, I wish to take you into my confidence and make one or two proposals. Firstly, I've bought a hotel up in Coates Crescent. You see...' Ginny now studied the diamond ring on her left hand, '...the big money I require for the like of this...' she raised her hand so that the gemstone winked at Sally, '...is made between the sheets.'

Sally was aghast. *Surely*, she thought, *Ginny, whom I always thought was shrewd but an upright businesswoman, isn't saying she's going into opposition with Dora Noyce! This can't be. This shouldn't be.*

Unaware of Sally's disapproval, Ginny went on, 'You see, my dear, the festival has taught me that hundreds, even thousands, of tourists, especially now that air travel is becoming cheaper and more frequent, will be coming to visit the Athens of the North – our Edinburgh – and I want to get in at the beginning of this boom. So it is my intention to start with one small hotel and build up from there.'

'Hotels,' exclaimed Sally, relaxing.

'Yes, tourist hotels. Full of people who'll wish to see the sights, visit the festival.'

Ginny now realised because Sally was laughing so loudly that she had thought that Ginny was going into the sex trade and she laughed too. 'Not in a thousand years would I ever consider that! But I'm going to put all my energies into the bed and breakfast trade. By the way, my smart hotel has a bar, but I won't be doing meals. No. No. Just a few well salted crisps and nuts on the tables to make my customers drouthie. Anyway, I have digressed, what all this means is I am going to give up being the licensee for my three pubs.'

Sally's face fell again.

'So what I am suggesting is...' Ginny deliberately allowed herself a long pause, '...that I take you up to the brewers, McEwan's, and suggest to them that they let you take over the tenancy.'

'Me – take over in here? Become the landlady!'

'Yes. And I'm going to speak to Mona about taking over in the King's Wark. Both of you have worked hard. You've changed these pubs from jungles to respectable watering holes. And the bonus is you have made more profit than was ever envisaged.'

'Well, I don't know. I do fancy working for myself, but will I need collateral?'

'If you mean the money up front for the stock, then I'm afraid you do.'

'That's a pity because I'd just got a deposit together for a flat in Gladstone Place, but I suppose...'

'In two years' times you'll have pocketed enough profit to buy a Gladstone Place flat outright.'

Five minutes passed by without either woman saying a word but thinking plenty.

Eventually Ginny, weighing every word before uttering it, spoke. 'I know there is no problem with you and Mona, but I, in all honesty, cannot recommend Carl to the brewers.'

'Are you saying you can't suggest that your manager in the Royal Stuart is fit to take over from you?'

'That I am.' Ginny stopped to ponder before confiding to Sally, 'You see, the upstart thinks my head buttons up the back and that I don't know that he's been ripping me off for years.'

'What?'

'He's a gambler, Sally. And he's been keeping McIntyre the bookies in Easter Road in luxury with the rake-off from my bar. So, here is my second proposition. How about I ask the brewers – and they will act on my recommendation – that you become their tenant there?'

'But how could I run two places?'

'Easy. You do what I did when I took you on. Train up someone who needs a job and their gratitude will keep them loyal to you. You already have an added bonus in that you have several very capable members of your family.'

'Oh Ginny, you have been so good to me. You picked me up when I was down and because of you I am able to let both Bobby and Helen stay on at school. And Helen has been accepted for teacher training at Moray House and next year Bobby will be applying to do law at Edinburgh University. He needs that. Not physically strong is my Bobby.'

Ginny had to hold her tongue. What she wanted to say was that Bobby was the strongest of her children, but he was expert at having Sally feel he needed her. Ginny liked Bobby too and she wished him well in his chosen career, and she also thought there might come a time when she needed a friendly lawyer at a discount price.

The clock on the wall told Sally it was nearly four o'clock. She was just thinking she should continue to sit here comfortably in the Four Marys rather than run home for a rest when an insistent thumping on the outside door alerted her. Jumping to her feet to answer the impatient summons, Sally called out, 'Just a minute. I'm no exactly Jack Flash.'

'Glad about that,' newly appointed Chief Inspector David Stock chortled when the door was opened to him.

Sally blushed. These days she not only felt like a love-struck teenager when she saw David Stock but also when she thought about him. So it had come as a relief to her that when he was promoted that he had been transferred to 'B' Division, whose headquarters were up in Gayfield Square. This meant he was no longer doing the rounds of the pubs in Leith and she wouldn't be bumping into him in the streets around the Shore.

Inviting David into the pub with a nod of her head and closing the door behind him, Sally asked, 'Is this a business call?'

Before answering, David took off his hat and sat down. 'Hmmm. Not really. You see, there was an attempted suicide…'

'If you are going to tell me about my brother Luke…'

David looked puzzled. 'Your brother Luke tried to commit suicide? Never. He's one of the best officers I have ever had under my command.'

'No. He didn't try to commit suicide; he saved Irish, who… Oh, never mind,' Sally said, waving her hand. 'Just get on with your story.'

'It was a woman. She was going to jump off the Scott Monument, but as she had been acting suspiciously a young cop followed her up and he managed to persuade her not to jump.'

'Persuaded her not to jump?'

'Well, okay – he had to punch her un-conscious or she would not only have leapt but as he was holding onto her she could have dragged him over as well. Confined space at the top, that is.'

'It certainly looks it from the ground.'

'Aye, and it makes such a mess in the gardens below when someone does land from a height, and it's also bad for tourism.'

Sally smiled. She knew the police had to have this warped sense of humour when dealing with the macabre or they would never get through.

'Anyway,' David continued. 'When we got her down, an ambulance took her to the Royal Infirmary and she's now in a locked ward. Spoke to her I did before the vehicle took off and she said...' David now took out his notebook from his top jacket pocket and began to read aloud,... '"I know you know Sally Stuart, so when you next see her tell her I'm sorry. Up till now I wasn't aware of how much grief I had caused her. And I am so pleased that she's stronger than me and never considered ending it all. Couldn't have lived with her doing that, no I couldn't." I hope you can work out from what I've told you who the lady is; because of confidentiality you know I cannot give you her name.'

'That's okay. I've worked it out for myself. Poor idiot.' Sally, whose feelings were mixed with anger, sadness and betrayal, paused briefly before saying, 'Suppose most will laugh at her and consider justice has been done and she has reaped what she sowed.'

'Will you go and visit her?'

'No.' Sally paused and chuckled. 'Do you know, David, this has been some blooming day for surprises.'

David nodded before standing up. 'I suppose I should be getting along,' he mumbled, 'but before...'

Sally looked up expectantly.

'I was just wondering ... that is, I have two tickets for the Charles Aznavour concert and my daughter was going to go with me but she's not keen on him. And she says she would rather stay with my wife...'

'How is your wife?'

David blew out his cheeks. 'It just not fair what's happening to her. She never complains and I know that she's riddled with guilt about the burden, as she sees it, the girls and I have to cope with. And do you know, we just wish it had been us that was stricken and not her.'

Talking about his wife's condition was obviously painful for David, so Sally quickly changed the subject. 'Back to Charles Aznavour,' she said. 'I wouldn't mind going with you on a strictly platonic basis.'

'Sally, I am a happily married man. I'm only asking you out for the night to use up the spare ticket. And as they are giving the tickets away, lots of other police officers and friends that you know will be there,' was David's quick reply.

No verbal response was forth coming from Sally, but silently she truthfully told herself, *Well, it's such a long time since someone was loving to me, and bed, especially, with you, would be wonderful, but I'll just have to settle for a date with conceited and over-rated Charles Aznavour and the rest of the Edinburgh Police Force.*

Sally needed to sleep, but slumber kept evading her. She hoped when her eyes did eventually close and she was comatose she could be spared going over the happenings of the day. After tossing and turning for two hours, she decided to get up and think about where she was going and who would be going with her.

Top of the priority list was straightening out the two tenancies. There was no doubt she would become landlady of both bars because of Ginny's backing. But being responsible for the two businesses would mean her running between the two pubs and therefore she would require a good, trustworthy manager in each. Josie was the obvious and good choice for the Four Marys, but where would she get a dependable, mature, hard-working person for the Royal Stuart?

Idly stirring the steaming-hot cocoa that she had made herself in the vain hope it would help her doze when she did go back to bed, she thought back to what Ginny had said about why she had helped her. 'You know Sally, you are always asking me why I helped you, trained you and showed you that I trusted you, and you think it was because of my sense of wrath about what Harry had done to you? No such thing. You see, I have found out that as you go through life, most of the people you give a hand up to, when they are down, repay you with loyalty and service. You are a prime example of this theory.' Ginny had stopped and looked about the bar. 'This bar has been dragged out of the pits by you, Sally, and made into a happy hostelry – a place where male and female customers can get good food and drink in clean and pleasant surroundings. Look,' Ginny went on whilst her hand swept the room, 'at what you achieved in three years. So remember when you're picking staff that family and then people who have a need will, not always though, be your best bet. They'll give you loyalty and peace of mind.'

Taking another sip of the comforting chocolate drink, Sally contemplated. What if she was to give Nancy the same chance that Ginny had given her? It would take her off the streets. Give her a purpose in life ... a reason to go on. There was a problem, though: she could not be serving behind the bar in the Four Marys. Sally giggled when she thought of how some of the bright sparks might kid the life out of Nancy by asking for 'a double Johnnie Walker and a quickie round the back'. Sally conceded that would never do, but putting her into the Royal Stuart was a good option. Nancy's notoriety wouldn't be well known there, and Sally could be assured that once she had her up and trained and left to get on with things that the place would be run properly by someone who, no matter what else, had intelligence, presence and personality.

Her next consideration was the family. She knew now she would be in a position to get a better house soon and that she would have no trouble supporting Helen and Bobby through college. Smirking, she acknowledged that her wee scams, which every licensed premises had, would more than pay for that. Harry was yesterday's news. In fact, she wouldn't have him back now. He had done her a favour. If he hadn't given her the push she would still be serving in the Co-op, and here she was a successful landlady. But it was Margo, her firstborn, who was breaking her heart. What had she done that had alienated her? She thought about her own relationship with Flora. There was no use thinking about Peggy: she had given her life, right enough, but she had been a cuckoo and had therefore never behaved in a motherly way towards any of her children except Daisy and Luke.

Now Flora was different. She was just so maternal that Sally knew no matter what she could rely on her. Had she not sided with her when Harry left? Sally felt hot tears begin to burn her eyes when her thoughts strayed again to Margo. She still couldn't believe Margo had been pregnant and had never told her – never cried out to her when her little boy was stillborn.

Sally had gone to the Eastern General Hospital Maternity Unit in Seafield and asked if she could see Margo. The duty nurse advised that that would not be possible because Margo already had three visitors at her bedside: her husband, her father and his friend. Throwing the bouquet of red roses into the bucket, Sally had just turned to leave when Johnny called out to her, 'Mrs Stuart, wait.'

'Why?' replied Sally.

'It's just that perhaps this is not the time for you and Margo to make up. I know you're sorry for all you didn't do for her...'

'Didn't do for her?' Sally cried. 'Now what else could I have done other than breathe for her?'

Johnny looked abashed. 'You know what Margo's like. If she has a mind to she could convince you the Crucifixion was just.'

Sally put her hand out to Johnny and he accepted it. He wasn't the lad she would have chosen for Margo. A bit on the glaikit side he was, but now she felt sorry for him. His life was difficult now. He was intelligent enough to work out the truth in everything, but he was unable to stand up to his domineering wife. 'If ever I can help you,' Sally managed to utter through her sobs, 'just

186

come to either of my two pubs. You won't have to explain, but I will give you all the help you need. By the way, only in the Four Marys and the Royal Stuart pubs, where I will soon be the landlady, am I still known as Mrs Stuart; everywhere else, and especially with family and friends, like you, it's plain Sally Mack.'

Margo knocked loudly on the door of the house her father now shared with Maggie, but there was no reply. It was true her father had distanced himself from her since she had announced that she was pregnant.

'Pregnant,' he had shrieked, putting up his hands as if to ward off an evil spell. 'Hey, don't you realise that will make me a grand-dad, and I'm much too young to be labelled that.'

This reaction had stumped Margo, who up till then had believed she was the light of her dad's life and anything she did would be welcomed by him. But now he was saying he didn't wish to be grandfather to his first grandchild – her first child. Why? But he had come to hold her hand when her baby had died.

Maggie, she remembered, had been delighted about the baby, and within days she was knitting matinee coats and bootees. It was while she was clicking away with the needles one evening that she timidly asked

Margo what her mother, Sally, had said about becoming a granny? Margo just shrugged her shoulders and coldly replied, 'Don't know. You see, I haven't bothered to tell her.'

Rapping hard on the door again, Margo wondered where Maggie could be. She had called in at the Co-op where she worked but no one seemed to know where she was today. The noise of Margo's knocking brought Maggie's neighbour, Mrs Tyree, to her door.

'Oh, it's you, Margo. You're wasting your time banging away there. Police called in last night and locked up the door. Seems Maggie was taken ill up the town and they carted her off to the hospital, or maybe the morgue. Wouldn't tell me what exactly had happened to her. But then that's the polis for you.'

Calling back a hasty thanks to Mrs Tyree, Margo sped out on to East Thomas Street and hailed a taxi. 'Royal Infirmary, driver,' she exclaimed and then sank back on the seat to relax.

At the hospital, Margo called at the Porter's Lodge and enquired after Maggie. The porter, dressed in his smart uniform, which assisted in buoying up his over-inflated ego, consulted his lists before informing Margo of the ward number, but before she could go into the main corridor he quickly added, 'Just hold on. That is a locked ward and I have to ring to see if you will be allowed entrance.'

'But,' spluttered Margo, 'it's my...' she hesitated before saying, '...my stepmother to be that I've come to see. She has no one but my dad and me.'

After consulting with the ward again, the porter nodded, 'It's okay. They've checked with Miss ... your stepmother to be and you can go on up.' He went on to give her directions to the ward and then cautioned, 'Wait by the entrance until someone comes to take you through.'

On arrival at the ward door, Margo was alarmed to see through the glass door that a male nurse was approaching with a bunch of keys. Selecting one, he unlocked the door and with a jerk of his head he indicated to Margo to come in, and he walked with her to Maggie's bed.

Margo just couldn't believe the frail, aged woman lying in the bed was Maggie. She was paler than death, and a bruise on her cheek along with several scratches on her forehead were quite alarming.

'What on earth happened?' Margo managed to splutter.

Wearily raising her hand, Maggie replied, 'Dinnae fret. I'd just had enough.'

'What? But you love my dad. And the ink is no quite dry on his divorce from my mum and when it does you and he will get married.'

'Don't you understand your dad's dumped

189

me for one of your auld classmates so I felt ... there was nothing left for me. Decided, I did, I'd be better out of it. Cannae stand being the laughing stock who got her comeuppance.'

'My dad's left you for one of my chums? Don't be daft, Maggie,' Margo cackled.

'But he has. And you know weeks ago, someone at work, who I was telling what I was going to wear at our wedding, told me he was singing duets with a young lassie. But I didn't believe her. Then your dad didn't come home two nights ago. So the following night I went up to that new club in Tollcross where he has been singing and...' Maggie started to sob quietly. 'And then I saw it for myself. Cuddling and fondling a lassie the same age as you. Brazen he was when I asked him to consider what he was doing. "Just come to my senses. I'm leaving you," was his quick reply.' Maggie was now crying uncontrollably. 'Even had ... the cheek ... to say I was past it and he wanted to spend the rest of his life waking up beside young Felicity...'

'Felicity. Oh no, not Felicity, behind the bike sheds at school, Gibson?'

'None other. So that's why I climbed the Scott Monument. Don't survive if you jump from there, you don't. But ... as luck would have it a young bobby came up to rescue me... Wish he hadn't bothered.'

'Oh Maggie, this cannot be true. My dad wouldn't make a fool of himself with someone like Felicity. No. Not my dad.' Margo stopped and leant over to hug Maggie.

Sally had given a lot of thought to the present she would like to give Ginny as a token of her gratitude. She would have liked to have presented her with another diamond ring, but that she could not afford. But what she could afford was a bottle of Chanel No. 5 – the expensive preferred fragrance of both Marilyn Monroe and Ginny. Whenever Sally was in Ginny's presence, she would inhale deeply and enjoy the wafting bouquet before promising herself that one day she too would smell sweet like Ginny.

The best place to purchase a bottle of Chanel was Jenners, the prestigious, world-famous department store on Princes Street, so Sally took herself there and asked the charming sales assistant for not one but *two* bottles of the fragrance. This was because she had decided that now she was a business lady she would have to give the right impression. At this moment in time she couldn't afford the mandatory mink jacket, but she could stretch to the aroma.

The perfume was also purchased because she had a date with David Stock and she wished to smell fragrant and not like an overflowing ashtray.

Funny, she thought, *that since going to work in the Four Marys I've got used to my clothes and hair stinking of smoke and alcohol, unlike Ginny, who always smells so sweet. But then Ginny has time to change her clothes twice daily, and her hair is washed and styled by the young up-and-coming hair stylist Charlie Miller at least three times every week. Wonder how much he charges?* Sally mused. *Could be*, she thought, *as he's just starting out and building up a clientele, not too much*. She then shook her head and her shoulders drooped as she pictured Ginny's new hairstyle. *That man is a genius and if I want to portray the right image I'll just have to afford him.*

Sally was surprised to find that the Charles Aznavour concert had not attracted a large audience. When it had been brought to the council's attention that only a few tickets had been sold, they decided to try and fill the theatre by offering free tickets to their staff and also included the police and fire service in the giveaway.

When Sally had taken her seat beside David, she was surprised to find that even the council's generosity had not resulted in anything like a full house. Charles was only into his first rendition when she appreciated why. By the third offering, David turned to her and said, 'Sorry about this. Do you fancy a drink in the Shakespeare bar across the road?'

'To be truthful, I don't normally drink alcohol,' was Sally's whispered response, 'but I could be persuaded to say yes – because I've been driven to it tonight.'

Sally had just got herself seated at a table when David returned from the bar with a large brandy for himself and an orange juice for her. Sitting down opposite her, he smiled before saying, 'Oh, by the way, did you change your mind and go up to the infirmary to see your...'

'No,' was Sally's abrupt reply. 'And I wish everyone would stop making me feel guilty – after all, she was the one who slapped me in the face.'

'Oh, oh,' was David's response. 'Didn't realise you held grudges.'

'Hold grudges?' Sally loudly exploded, causing other nearby customers to look towards her. 'Let me tell you, I don't stick pins in wax effigies or keep shrunken heads...' jumping to her feet she continued, '...but, believe me, I'm not stupid enough to put my head on the block again. So could I bid you goodnight.' With that, she flounced out the door and hailed a taxi.

'Where to, lady?' the cab driver asked.

Sally hesitated. 'Suppose if I am to get some peace in this world it had better be the Royal Infirmary.'

The taxi drew to a halt at the main entrance to the 1920s upgraded Royal Infirmary of Edinburgh and Sally alighted.

After paying the taxi fare, she looked up at the world-famous clock tower that dominated the centre of the sprawling building and was surprised to see it was already ten o'clock. *Well past visiting hours*, she reminded herself. Her eyes were then drawn to the stones on either side of the clock face and she noted that the inscription on the left read, 'I WAS A STRANGER AND YE TOOK ME IN', and on the right, 'I WAS SICK AND YE VISITED ME'. 'Right enough.' Sally paused to have a little laugh before going on to whisper audibly, 'Could have been written for my pal and me these comforting words because, like it says, she was a stranger and I took her in and befriended her, but my reward was not gratitude... Regrettably it was betrayal that made me sick. And sick as I was, she never visited me. And as to the second dedication, that fits too, because am I not here to visit her?' Sally hesitated before acknowledging that she was indeed calling in on her – but regrettably with no Christian charity in her heart.

Without any further deliberation, she proceeded up the steps, which took her into the main corridor. Immediately she was confronted with two large panels bearing the names of those who had donated to the upgrade of this medical institution in 1920. She noted they were mostly from the Scottish nobility, business owners and those wealthy people who valued having their names promoted.

Turning to glance at another panel in the hope that it would give her directions to the ward, she was pleased to see that it did.

The sudden appearance of a creaking trolley caused her to turn with a start, and she gasped when she found herself face to face with a porter who was pushing a shroud-covered portable table. 'No need to be feart, missus,' the man lisped. 'Sure, it's no the dead you hae to fear, it's the twisted living.'

Sally nodded in agreement before starting towards the stairs to the upper wards. The loud clicking of her heels on the stone steps, however, seemed to her, who was trying to sneak into a ward unnoticed, to be heralding her arrival.

The door to the ward she sought was locked, but as luck would have it, John Thomson, the constable on the opposite shift from Luke, was emerging. 'Well, hello,' he exclaimed when faced with Sally. 'What are you doing here at this time of night?'

Sally gave a nervous little laugh. She liked John Thomson and it was evident he liked Josie, Luke and herself, always stopping them to ask how they were doing and how they were getting on. 'Visiting a friend,' Sally managed to mumble when she stopped her deliberations. However, before going on she placed a hand intimately on his arm. 'You see, I explained,' she lied, 'to the duty staff I couldn't make the normal visiting hour tonight – you know, John, how I have to keep the punters from dying of thirst – so they said I could have a few minutes now – provided, that is, she's not asleep.'

John stood aside and allowed Sally to enter. 'Aye, well, I would have waited for you and given you a lift hame, but we're busy tonight and I'm only up here because a punter decided to go for a swim in the docks.' He chuckled before continuing, 'Cannae get any help from the other divisions; they're all hard-pressed too. And into the bargain we had to police a big concert in the Usher Hall. That French bloke ye ken the singer Charlie something or other.'

'Aznavour, or as we say in Leith, Asnovoice,' was Sally's response as she removed her shoes so she could tiptoe into the ward.

'Listen, Sally, for a long time now I've been thinking of bringing in my dad to meet you. Knew your mother, he did, and he was wondering if you or anybody in your family had taken after her.'

Hope not, Sally thought before looking up into John's eyes and replying, 'I would love to meet your dad so bring him in any time you like.'

In the second bed on the right, quite a distance from the nurses' station, which indicated that the person in the bed was no longer critical, Sally found her quarry. She was awake.

'Is that really you?' was the patient's hoarse, whispered question to Sally, who took up a position at the foot of the bed.

'Yes, Maggie, it's me. And what I want to know is why have you been upsetting my apple cart again?' hissed Sally.

'Oh Sally, he left me. Can you believe after all I did for him that he could throw me over for a *bimbo*?' Maggie began to sob quietly.

Sally, her head spinning, didn't reply because she was thinking, *But Maggie, you were only with him for three years – how do you think I felt that after twenty plus years looking after him and bearing him three bairns that he waltzed off with you, a has-been that never was?*

Sensing, as she thought, Sally's grief, Maggie broke the silence. With great sympathy, she mumbled, 'Sally, I'm sorry I hurt you... I've missed you so much... Especially now I'm all alone. I am truly, truly sorry I stole Harry from you.'

Lifting Maggie's right hand into hers, Sally squeezed it hard. 'No. No. You should have no regrets about taking Harry from me.'

Pulling her hand from Sally's so she could

struggle up in bed, Maggie leant closer to Sally. 'I just know,' she confided quietly, 'he'll come to his senses and he'll leave her and come back – and if he wants to go to you then that will be okay by me.'

Having become a tough woman over the last three years, Sally knew she had to respond forcibly to Maggie's statement so, having no regard for the other sleeping patients, she announced in a loud voice, 'I don't think you understand, Maggie, that I'm here not to try and get Harry back but to thank you most sincerely for having taken him off my hands. You see, him going liberated me, and now I wouldn't take him back even if he came with his backside studded in diamonds.'

Sally could go on no further with her tirade, as the duty nurse had flown like a ghost silently down the ward. Grabbing Sally by the arm, she demanded, 'Who on earth are you? And what are you doing here?'

'It's alright, nurse,' Maggie croaked. 'She's my best friend and she has just told me that she's going to look after me.'

'Is that right?' the nurse asked.

'No. Not really. I just came by to say to Maggie not to worry. Plus, I think you should get her some treatment for her delusions.'

'But Sally, you will say that you'll take me out of here or I won't get out.'

Sally turned on her heel and headed for the door. The nurse unlocked it and before closing it on Sally she said, 'She's being transferred to the Andrew Duncan Clinic.'

Sighing and sobbing gently, the supposedly tough Sally sagged against the wall. *Am I hearing right?* she wondered. *Did that nurse, in a coded form, say that Maggie has been sectioned for her own protection and now she is being transferred to the Royal Edinburgh psychiatric hospital? Oh,* Sally thought, *Why, Harry, do you and your blasted daughter Margo think you have the right to drive other people insane?*

It was going on eleven when Sally emerged from the hospital, and when a spectral male figure emerged from the shadows she became alarmed. What could she do? Her first thought was to run towards the front street, where she reckoned there would be someone to assist her. She was just on the verge of bolting when the man said, 'Somehow I knew you would come here.'

She stopped abruptly and turned to face him. 'And how did you know, for definite, I would be here, David?'

'The taxi driver returned to his rank too soon to have dropped you in Leith, so I asked him where he had put you down.'

'And he told you,' Sally exclaimed.

'To be truthful, he wouldn't have, but a

flash of a warrant card loosened his tongue. So now may I drive you home?'

Sally was tempted to say 'no' but thought better of it, and soon they were making their way to her home.

Once they had parked, David turned to her. 'Look, Sally,' he confided, 'all I want is to have you as a friend who will accompany me to the theatre, pictures and whatever – please believe that my intentions are honourable.'

'But surely you have numerous colleagues who could do the arts round with you?'

'Oh, I have a lot of mates, but their interests are in football, bowling, fishing and any other sport they fancy.'

'I see.'

'So is that a "yes"?'

'No. It's a definite "no". You see, going to the hospital to see Maggie reminded me of how awful and worthless I felt when Harry left me. And what kind of a person would I be if I was to do that to another woman – especially one who is facing the problems that your wife is?'

'But Elspeth is always saying that I must try to make a life for myself that doesn't include her.'

'Yes. That is what she knows she must say. But somewhere deep down in her psyche she is hoping that you still love her – find her attractive – will be the one holding her hand when her premature end comes.'

'You don't know Elspeth. Honestly, since she was diagnosed with that blasted multiple sclerosis she's been urging me to divorce her.'

'And leave your daughters to struggle to care for her ... pick up your burden? I don't think so.'

David shook his head. 'I would never do that. Believe me, when Elspeth's end does come, she will know that I thank her, most sincerely, for the two most precious gifts she gave me – my daughters. She will also leave us knowing that always I will be grateful to her for having been my beautiful, loving wife.'

'And that is how it should be. As to us ... you're welcome at any time to come into the Four Marys for a dram and a chat, but that's all. Platonic at the start we could be, but after a time, because we are both sexually attracted to each other...'

David scoffed and shook his head.

'Shake your head all you like,' Sally responded, 'but there's no use in denying it. After all, is that not why you came to look for me tonight?'

'But our relationship *will* be on a strictly idealistic basis.'

'Even if it was, the rest of the world won't see it like that. What they will think is that I'm a tart who's having an affair with a married man and that would never be acceptable to me.'

'Surely if you know it's not true then you could cope.'

Sally shook her head. 'Don't you also realise your career promotion prospects would then be non-existent?'

'That's rubbish.'

'No, it's not. John Knox may have been dead for hundreds of years, but he still lives and rules in all the headquarters in the High Street.'

David did not respond, because he knew she was speaking the truth. At this moment in time, his career meant so much to him that he just wouldn't put it in jeopardy.

Sally interrupted his thoughts. 'Besides,' she began, 'the other thing I have been reminded of today is how I hated the bloody awful reputation my mother had. Jump into bed with any man, she would. So David, you must accept that I will never embarrass my children in that way. Oh no, no one will ever be able to say that Sally Mack is just like her mother.'

She said no more, but she did think that if she ever did, and she doubted if she ever would, forget to be virtuous it would be with a man like David Stock.

When Sally met up with Nancy to put forward her proposal, Nancy's reaction was totally different from what she had expected.

'Sally,' Nancy had begun, 'it's not that I'm not flattered that you thought of me to help you out. It's just that I have been self-employed all my life. Right enough, I sign on every week saying I'm available for work, but I never ask for any unemployment benefit; I just need my card stamped so I can get the state old age pension when I'm sixty.'

Sally was dumbfounded and unable to hide her incredulity, so all she could say was, 'What?'

'Och, Sally, surely you cannae be that nave. Naw. Naw. There's no one single pro, like me, paying the government its due in tax and insurance. So you see I wouldnae be working for myself any more and not only would I then be paying income tax but I would have to pitch up every day even if I didnae feel like getting up.'

'So you don't want either the training or the job?'

'No saying exactly that. And it's true that at my age it might be a step in the right direction.' Nancy now advanced closer to Sally and lifted her right hand and waggled her fingers before cheekily asking under her breath, 'And as part of the deal ... does a compulsory mink jacket and diamond rings come with it?'

Shaking her head, Sally was about to withdraw her offer, but she looked hard at Nancy and she saw that her stance was just a bluff.

She could see in her face that Nancy wanted nothing more than to be out of her sordid profession and here was Sally offering a way of getting a bit of respectability. But what she didn't want was Sally knowing how hard life was getting for her on the streets, especially now that she was past her best. No longer was she able to pick and choose her clients like the young lassies could. And the day was just around the corner when there would only be the likes of drunken Sam, who would proposition her for the price of a glass of cheap wine. 'Well, Nancy,' Sally said when the pause had gone on too long, 'you think my very good offer over and remember it would require you completely giving up your present trade. Now should you decide to accept my terms of employment, just turn up on Monday at the Royal Stuart at ten o'clock sharp.'

'Ten o'clock in the morning? That's the middle of the night.'

'Aye, for you right now it is,' agreed Sally, thinking, *But if there's any justice in the world soon you'll be, like me, tucked up in bed by midnight with nothing other than a big mug,* she giggled, *of cocoa.*

When Nancy, who had not only scrubbed up well but was also suitably attired in a Burberry coat, made her grand entrance into the Royal Stuart pub, Sally knew she had done the right thing. *Oh yes*, Sally mused, *I may have had to drag her up on to her feet and be her crutch, but I can see today from her demeanour she will soon be walking unaided.*

Sally was right, because Nancy, whose life should have rendered her senseless, was a quick learner and within three hectic months Sally could confidently leave her to run the Royal Stuart. Granted, her idea of gourmet lunches was serving Heinz Tomato Soup along with Hannah the Brunswick Street home baker's lukewarm famous Scotch pies and sausage rolls, but it appeared that was what the working men seemed to appreciate, along, of course, with a pint of McEwan's Best.

On arrival at the registry office, Harry couldn't believe how many of his adoring fans had turned up. It had not dawned on him that 'his fans' were mostly in their teens or early twenties, like his twenty-four-year-old bride.

Felicity had insisted that, as it was bad luck for the groom to see the bride before the ceremony, she should arrive with her dad. As the limousine drew up in front of the registry, the crowd began to surge forward when Felicity's father, dressed in morning clothes, emerged from the car. Bowing to the crowd, he then offered his hand to his daughter, and when the audience saw how young and beautiful she looked, they gasped. Here was their star dressed in a knee-length white taffeta dress and instead of a veil she had donned a sparkling tiara on her ash-blonde hair. Leith had never seen such opulence. Standing quite still so everyone could enjoy the spectacle, Felicity smiled and waved. Soon her audience were screaming, 'Felicity, Felicity, sing us a song.'

Feigning modesty, she simpered, 'Now, now, this is my wedding day so it's you who should be singing to me.'

A young fan immediately jumped forward, and kneeling on the pavement he grabbed hold of Felicity's hand and began to warble 'I'm Walking Behind You on Your Wedding Day'. However, when the twitter drifted into the registry office Harry thought that the laddie was definitely off-key and that he had sung it so much better to Margo on her wedding day.

No one would ever be sure of what went through Felicity's head at that moment, but she bent down and helped the young lad to his feet. 'Thank you, Billy,' was all she could mumble as her eyes sought her dad.

Margo, dressed in a deep-pink satin creation that made her look quite elegant, tottered forward on her four-inch high heels. 'Come on, Felicity. My dad's waiting.'

The horror of the word 'dad' spoken by Margo had an effect upon Felicity. 'That's right, you're the same age as me, and my intended is your father. Not only that, he's older than my dad. Dad, I need you,' she screamed, scanning the crowd for her father.

Wondering what all the commotion was about, Harry emerged into the street and strode over to Felicity. Following him, an attendant said, 'Could I remind you that the registrar is waiting and there will another wedding in half an hour.' Placing a hand on both Felicity and Harry, he continued, 'So, Miss, if you and your father...' he scanned the crowd and then beckoned to Billy, '...and you too if you still want to get married today, just follow me.'

Billy laughed and encouraged the spectators to join in the hilarity. Felicity's dad did manage to fight his way through the mob, and when he got towards his daughter, he asked, 'Is there a problem, love?'

Felicity nodded and managed to mumble through racking sobs, 'Oh Dad, you're right: in a couple of years he'll be like old age creeping over me. Oh Dad, please tell me what to do.'

Harry was taken aback. This humiliation was not what he had expected. So, grabbing Felicity by the arm, he began to propel her towards the registry entrance. 'Look,' he snarled, 'don't you dare make me look a right charlie. We're getting married today and you can sue for a divorce after I give you a right good doing tonight.'

'Dad, save me,' screeched Felicity. 'He's going to thump me.'

'That'll be the day,' retaliated Felicity's father, before punching Harry on the nose.

Next thing Harry knew, Mr Gibson had called on the wedding car to come and take him and his daughter home. Before they left, Harry thought that Mr Gibson was going to give the customary pour-out of coins to the assembled children, but instead he called Billy over and gave him a fistful of folding money. 'Well done, son,' he declared whilst slapping Billy on the back. 'Couldn't have done it better myself.' Waving to the crowd, he then jumped into the car and was spirited away.

'Oh Dad,' Margo sobbed. 'What are you going to do? The house has been sold and you can't stay with Felicity or Maggie any more... You have nowhere to live.'

'Margo, you couldn't?'

She shook her head. 'No. There's no room for you at my house.' Stopping to consider what could be done, she exhaled before saying, 'And Maggie's in bedlam, but I suppose I could ask Mum... But she probably won't.'

'Well, in that case there's nothing else I can do but catch the train to Inverness and find out if my mother will put me up until people have stopped laughing.'

Margo nodded. 'Okay. But I think I should

do you a favour and have a long-overdue word with Mum.'

Saturday lunchtime was, as always, a busy time for the Four Marys. As luck would have it, Sally was on duty, assisted by Rita. The soup of the day, according to Rita, was vegetarian lentil, made with some good ham bones but of course with no meat on them.

Sally had just finished advising the kitchen of the latest orders when Margo came up to the bar. 'Want something?' was Sally's non-committal enquiry.

'Mum, I know you'll be sorry to know that Dad has been ... jilted.'

Trying hard to control her sniggers, Sally replied, 'That right? And they say there's no justice.'

'I know, Mum. You *are*, like me, so sorry that he has been so humiliated. Imagine, being dumped like an old pair of shoes.'

Sally wanted to say, 'Good. Now he knows how it feels when someone grips your heel.' However, all she uttered was, 'And Margo, now if you don't mind I'm busy – very busy.'

'Mum, I know you are, but we have to talk about Dad.'

'Look, if by that you mean you're here to ask me to give him a bed then the answer is no. Positively no.' And as she didn't wish to wash any more of her dirty linen in public, she said no more, but she did fix an insincere smile on her face.

Her grin, however, genuinely grew when David Stock arrived, and she was sweeter than honey when she asked him, 'What's your pleasure, David? And could I introduce you to my daughter, Margo. She just dropped in to give me some good news.'

'How do you do,' David said, offering Margo his hand. 'And Sally, I've just popped in for a dram and a chat.'

'Oh, surely you mean take me to the pictures. But as I've just seen Josie off for a week's holiday, could I take a rain check? But in the meantime, let me treat you to a double Glenmorangie.'

David didn't know what Sally was talking about, so he just nodded and took a seat at a table. Giving a sideways glance to Margo, he thought she seemed crestfallen, and when she said to her mother, 'So there is no room in your life for my dad?' he didn't know why but he was very pleased.

Sally shook her head. 'Know something, Margo? I just have time for those who have never broken my heart.'

Scalding tears were now spilling down Margo's cheeks. Sniffing loudly, she blubbered, 'Mum, I'm so sorry. You see I now know how wrong I have been.' She halted to wipe her cheeks before adding, 'What I'm saying is, please could you allow me to come back into your life?'

Sally nodded. What else does a mother do other than with delight follow the Bible and take the prodigal back.

Flora and Shonag were seated on the garden bench that overlooked the Moray Firth. They had reached the sunset stage in life when at the end of the day it felt just right to relax and enjoy reminiscing.

The two women had been born in this now subdivided house. Their adult lives had not been free from problems – Shonag had a son who was shunned by the strict brethren she was a member of just because he was homosexual, and Flora had the heartache of knowing that her son was a womaniser and a blood-sucking parasite. However, as they watched the sun set they could recall the happy days of their childhood when all they knew was security, warmth and, most importantly, love in abundance.

'We got a little bit done today,' Shonag observed while shielding her eyes from the glorious rays of the setting sun.

'Suppose so,' replied Flora, 'but know something, Shonag – it takes me longer to think about doing some work nowadays than it used to take me to do it.'

Both chuckled before an easy, comfortable silence fell between them. Still protecting her eyes, Shonag looked down to the winding pathway that brought you up to the houses.

'Here,' she said, grabbing Flora's arm. 'Is that a stranger that's coming our way?'

Lifting her left hand to her forehead, Flora stared down the road. Jumping up, she shouted, 'My old eyes don't think it's a stranger. Look at his gait. It's either your William or my Harry.'

The women kept watch on the road until they saw that the man was Harry. Starting to run towards him, Flora shouted, 'It's my laddie. Oh please, God in heaven, don't let him be bringing me bad news.'

Once Harry was safely in Flora's house and Shonag had departed to her own home to fetch some scones she had baked, Flora slowly drawled, 'What brings you?'

Harry sank into the old, comfortable armchair that had once been his grandfather's domain – his, and only his, province, where he had reigned supreme. 'Mum,' Harry mumbled as he sniffed, 'I've been jilted.'

Flora erupted into uncontrollable laughter.

'You might think it's funny, but it was at the registry office that she ditched me. The laughing stock of the whole of Leith I am.'

'Good for her. Besides, she was not for you.'

Harry shrugged before asking, 'Mum, can I stay here for two weeks?'

'Yes, but you'll have to work in the gardens.'

Harry looked down at his hands. *Mine are*

212

the hands of a gentleman – not a labourer.
Felicity and Maggie always said what gentle
sensitive hands I have, but what will they think
of them after two weeks grafting up here? But,
he conceded, *that is not my biggest problem: it*
is getting back to having a woman in my life.
Felicity is gone and won't be coming back.
Maggie... Well, she just doesn't fit my image
now. And Sally ... well? Suddenly he sat bolt
upright before speaking to his mother again.
'Mum,' he wheedled, 'you're on such good
terms with Sally, is there any possibility you
would ask her to take me back?'

Flora's mouth fell open.

Harry, unaware that he had shocked his
mother, continued, 'She's doing well for
herself. And I could do a lot better for myself by getting hitched to her again and taking over her businesses. And she will let me.'

'Aye, and more fool her.' Flora paused and
was pensive before adding, 'Right enough,
I'm your mother and I can't shut my door
on you, but Sally,' she laughed gleefully, 'she
now knows for certain you were a millstone
round her neck and no way will she ever let
you sponge off her again – and if she ever
does, I'll have her certified.'

Harry's reply was to laugh raucously.
'Mum, you think you know Sally. Believe me,
you don't even begin to comprehend what
makes her tick. Do you know when I told her
I was leaving her she fell down on her knees

213

and begged me to stay? Still grovelling, she pleaded...' Harry now cruelly imitated Sally's distraught voice, '..."Oh Harry, you are my life. Please, please always remember you can come back home any time and I will welcome you with open arms."'

Harry paused before continuing in his own voice, 'Had the cheek then to try and blackmail me by sobbing, "Darling, have you thought about how you'll be destroying our children's happiness?" So you see, you're wrong, Mother, and in a few weeks' time I'll be running the Four Marys and the Royal Stuart and have my feet firmly tucked beneath Sally's table, where she will be delighted to have them.'

'You think so? Well, I'm a better judge of character than you and I say no way, sonny boy, will she have you back. So you'd better go and find yourself another bimbo.'

Two weeks later at afternoon closing time, Harry strolled into the Four Marys bar. Rita, who was busy washing glasses in the bar sink whilst Sally was cashing up, whispered, 'Don't spin around right now, Sally, but a bar of chocolate that would like to eat itself has just walked in.'

Sally stopped counting, but she did not about turn.

'Hello, Sally. Long time no see,' a voice purred.

Sally didn't need to turn around to see who was speaking. She knew that voice so well. That voice that used to make her feel weak at the knees. That voice that would whisper in her ear when he wanted her to do something for him. And whatever he'd wanted, she'd granted.

Banging the till drawer shut, she swivelled slowly round, and picking up a damp cloth, she started to mop up the spills from the counter whilst she looked Harry straight in the eyes. 'And what do you want?' she asked, as she noted he had gone to the trouble of dressing himself up. However, the silk cravat, his Brycreemed hair and the aroma of the cologne he liked to splash about himself only served to make her shudder.

'To start with, a double malt on the house to celebrate,' he drawled as he winked at her.

Rita had gone over to the optic, but a warning glare from Sally had her stop in her tracks. 'Sorry, Harry,' Sally sweetly but firmly began, 'but you're barred in here and at the Royal Stuart too.'

'Barred? But you don't understand I'm here to answer your prayers? I'm coming back to you.'

'You're what?' Sally exclaimed.

'I know you're surprised, but I'm belatedly taking up your offer to come back to you. Oh Sally dear, I want to make life easier for you.

I could take over the responsibility...' Harry now waved his arms about to embrace the whole of the room before adding, '...of all this off your shoulders. Now does that not excite you, Sally?'

'As a matter of fact, the thought of you coming back into my life fills me with dread!'

'Are you mad? I'm offering to come back to you. Be your loving husband and partner again.'

'And I'm saying could you please leave right now. You see, you're making my nice saloon look cheap and gaudy. What I am saying is, I wish you to get out of my sight. You're a loser, a sponger, a no user, a yesterday's man, and as far as I'm concerned you can go forth and multiply!'

'And that goes for me too,' Rita added with gusto before she skipped across the floor and opened the door wide for Harry to pass through. 'And,' Rita, who had not been introduced to Harry, called out to his retreating form, 'I would like to have said it was a pleasure to meet you, but it wasn't and I wouldn't have been as polite as Sally and told you to go forth and multiply, I would simply have said, "Why don't you fu–"'

'Rita!' Sally's voice reverberated towards her. 'Language, language.'

5

1967

'Know something, Rita?'

'No till you tell me, Sally.'

'It's just that I didnae realise how much of a load Josie takes off my shoulders,' Sally confided as she looked about the pristine part of the saloon bar.

'Hope you're no grudging her a holiday?'

'No! I'm just saying that she's fair settled in here and done a good, very good, job.'

'Right enough, she's taken to running the Four Marys like a duck takes to water.'

'Aye, and you've done your bit too.' Sally nodded before adding, 'And as you know, I like to give credit where credit's due, and between the two of you not only have you got this place on the map but you've also added a bit of class.'

'Here, talking of getting this place on the map, what do you think of this?' Rita paused, pursed her lips and nodded before continuing. 'Your Josie had just left yesterday for her holiday when this young lassie came in. Foreigner she is.'

'What nationality?'

'Dinnae ken, because I just couldnae place

her accent. She does speak English, but it has a sort of drawl to it. Anyway, she said to me as she nursed a gin and tonic, "The woman who runs this place: what's her name?" I answered Mrs Stuart and quickly added but she's no looking for any staff at the moment. Got quite agitated about that she did, but then she blurted out, "That's okay. I'm no looking for a job, but I was wondering if Mrs Stuart's maiden name was Mack?" And I was just about to answer her when in comes your brother in full uniform. "It's three o'clock, Rita," he shouted so that all the customers could hear him. "Drink up," I said, "this officious bobby here is telling me it's time to put the shutters up." Anyway, as I was walking the lassie to the door, which your brother, without my permission, had locked, I told her your maiden name was Mack and you would be on duty tonight.'

'Can't think of who that might be?' Sally mused while searching her memory. 'An old classmate?' she absently speculated. 'Naw, it couldn't be someone I was at school with, because I was hardly ever there. Anyway, it doesn't matter. I won't have to wait long to find out – hope she's no expecting free hospitality.'

Rita didn't reply. Firstly, she had bad feelings about this lassie and she hoped she wouldn't end up being bad news. Secondly, she conceded that Sally was very generous to family, friends and staff, but she could be quite tight where strangers were concerned.

Josie, who had never been out of Britain, was bowled over by the beauty of Menorca. The travel agent in Queensferry Street had gone out of his way to promote the island. He'd told Josie he had been there himself last year and he was going again this year. He recommended the resort of Santo Tomas as a place that was still not, and he thought never would be, spoilt by over-development and tourism.

Leaning back at the beach bar, Josie allowed the sun to warm her face and her sangria to relax her. *This is sheer heaven*, she thought, and was so unlike the life she had had. She grew pensive. Here she was at thirty-seven still single. True, she had really enjoyed her life in the last three years. Running the Four Marys had boosted her confidence, and because Sally valued her efforts, she was paid a good wage. If it had not been the case, she would never have been able to afford this holiday and to stay in the four-star Santo Tomas hotel.

She had been picked up at the airport by a limousine: no tourist bus for the clients of the posh Santo Tomas Hotel. A porter had taken care of her luggage and the next time she saw it it was sitting in her room. All the splendour made her feel as if she was at last recognised in her own right as a successful lady.

Glancing along the beach, she saw in the distance there were cranes. She worked out that building was going on there and she decided that tomorrow, if she felt like it, she would go and see what was going on.

She was surprised when she arrived at the site to find that they were building luxury flats and that the sales office was not only close by but also open for business.

She would never know why she decided to enquire of the saleswoman as to when the flats would be finished and how much they would cost. But she did.

In broken English, the lady was pleased to furnish Josie with the details. 'The date for the completion of the flats,' she began, 'is only three months away. And it was hoped to have them furnished and ready for habitation by the buyers three months later, which would be in time for the next year's holiday periods.'

'Hmmm,' was all Josie could manage to say.

The woman, who appeared not to notice Josie's reluctance, continued, 'One-bedroom flats will cost around five thou...'

With a disarming smile that belied her panic, Josie interrupted, 'No use going on about the other flats. It's a one-bedroom flat on the third floor – preferably the end one – that I am interested in.'

'But,' the saleswoman retaliated, 'the pent-house flats have three bedrooms and three bathrooms and when you stand on the balcony you are able to see over to Majorca.'

'Granted,' was Josie's quick reply, 'but the one-bedroom flat is what my sister and I can afford and the view of the Mediterranean Sea will suit us just fine. So what's the deposit on the one-bedroom flat that is situated on the third floor, and if that's not available, the second? I also require to be advised on when the capital sum will be due.'

Josie had intended to ring Sally at least once during her holiday, but when she got back to the hotel after haggling with the saleswoman she experienced dual emotions. First she felt elated that within Sally's and her grasp was a holiday flat on the Med – and wouldn't she be the envy of all her pals in the launderette? Second was the sheer panic that had arisen in her when she really considered how much of a shock it would be to Sally and, indeed, would canny Sally be prepared to come up with most of the money?

The Four Marys bar was busier than usual for a Friday night, and Sally had coerced Margo, who was capable of pulling a pint, into helping out.

Just after nine, when things were quietening down, as revellers made their way to the Assembly Rooms dance hall, Sally went over to

221

speak to David, who had popped in for a double malt.

'You were very busy tonight,' David observed.

Chuckling, Sally replied, 'Aye. And here was me thinking that as beer has gone up to ten pence a pint that nobody would have a thirst.'

Their conversation continued, and they spoke about this and that and everything and nothing. She was so engrossed in the banter that she didn't notice a distraught Helen rushing into the bar.

'My mother,' Helen sniffing and choking cried. 'Margo, where is Mammy? I just have to get hold of her.'

'Just stop the hysterics, Helen. Our mum is over there,' replied Margo, who had always thought that her sister was an overindulged prima donna.

Without another word being spoken, Helen turned and rushed towards Sally. 'Oh Mum, you've got to come. Our Bobby has had an accident – a bad accident.'

Sally's hand flew to her mouth. Rising to flee, she asked, 'Where is he? What happened?'

'Oh Mum, you see Bobby and I went over to Leith Hospital to wait for Daisy finishing. We intended...'

'For heaven's sake, will you hurry up and get to what's happened,' Sally yelled.

'I am getting there. Be patient,' was a tearful Helen's reply. 'It was like this: we were all going to the dancing, and while we were waiting for...'

Helen could see her mother was getting very agitated, so she just blurted, 'Look, a wee boy on a guider came hurtling down the pavement on Mill Lane and knocked Bobby over ... Mum... His bad leg is broken!'

'Helen, for God's sake, where is my son?'

'In Leith Hospital. Did you not hear me say we were standing waiting for Daisy to finish her shift?'

Sally did not reply. But as she was just five minutes away from her son, who she knew would be requiring her support, she started for the door.

'Mum,' hollered Margo, 'you can't leave me to run the shop. I don't know what to do.'

Drawing up abruptly, Sally turned towards the bar. 'Margo,' she bellowed, 'it's quarter past nine. The busy time is over. Clear up and at ten o'clock throw any customers still in here out on their backsides and then lock the door! Honestly, Margo, can't you ever think for yourself?'

'That's unfair, Mum. And do you think I should come up to the hospital after I close up here...? Mum, I really don't know what to do,' Margo called out to the retreating form of her mother.

223

At a quarter to ten, the pub had two customers left in it. Then the door opened and in breezed a young woman who Margo judged to be in her late teens or very early twenties.

'What can I get you?' Margo asked as she ran a wet cloth over the bar.

'Well, if I have to have a drink I'll have a … Pimm's No. 1.'

Margo, while making up the exotic drink, was able to eye the lassie up. She didn't know why, but she thought the young woman was somewhat familiar and reminded her of someone – but try as she might she wasn't able to put a finger on whom. Laying down the drink and receiving payment, Margo smiled before asking, 'You a stranger in these parts?'

'Yes. I'm just trying to catch up with Mrs Stuart. I was told she'd be on duty tonight.'

'She was, but a pressing family problem had her leave in a hurry – and unfortunately that meant I was left in charge here,' Margo informed the young woman, waving her hand about to indicate the mess that Sally had left her in.

'Oh,' exclaimed the young woman, 'not only is she a traitor but a coward as well.'

Margo's mouth fell open and she pondered as to who this pretty, young, vivacious woman, who obviously hated her mother so much, could be. Deciding that she had to come quickly to her mother's defence, she replied, 'Let me tell you – now what is your name?'

'Angela.'

'Then, Angela, let me tell you that my mother is a hardworking woman and she has raised my brother, sister and me very well. Very well indeed.'

Angela's spontaneous laugh echoed around the saloon. 'Did she now? Know something? I'm really pleased for you that over the years she managed to find a sense of responsibility.'

The clock loudly chiming ten reminded Margo that she must lock up now. Turning to Angela, she said, 'You will have to leave now, but come back – let's say in three days' time. My mum should have everything under control by then.'

Slipping graciously from the stool, Angela smiled broadly. However, wide as the smile was, it didn't reach her eyes. 'That's a date then,' she drawled, pausing to wickedly lick her lips. 'And would you tell your *beloved mother* it doesn't matter how much she tries to avoid me, I have every intention of confronting her.'

Sally, lost in her own private thoughts, did not acknowledge the greeting from the hospital porter, Mr Malone.

Striding past him and taking the steps on

her right two at a time, she arrived in the casualty department. Immediately she enquired of a staff nurse where her son Bobby was, quickly correcting his name to Robert Stuart.

'At the present moment your son's condition is being assessed by the consultant surgeon, who will speak to you as soon as he has completed his examination.'

'How much longer will that take?' an impatient Sally demanded.

The nurse had now been joined by the officious sister in charge, who made it evident she was the one Sally should be speaking to. Before replying to Sally, the sister said, 'Thank you, Nurse Smith, I will attend to Mrs Stuart.'

Once the nurse had departed, the sister then turned to Sally. 'Mrs Stuart,' she began in clipped tones, 'the examination of your son's injuries will take as long as necessary. So could I suggest you sit down...' she then pointed to the corridor, '...out there until I call you back.'

Cowed by the authority that rested within the woman, Sally immediately turned and found herself a seat.

Half turning the chair, so she could see the consulting-room door, Sally then sank down on it. Already her thoughts were fully consumed with the memories of Bobby's childhood. Firstly she recalled how she had cried when she was told he had a deformity. It turned out it was only that one leg was slightly shorter than the other. Sniffing, she could in her mind's eye see him learning to walk and stumbling and tumbling but never crying. She was broken-hearted for him, but he behaved as if everybody had a shortness of something. A few years later, Davidovich, a Polish refugee, had come into her life and he was able to expertly cobble Bobby's shoes so he walked evenly. She had lost count of the number of attempts the Princess Margaret Rose Hospital had tried to fix his shoes and, okay, they were fine, but not as perfect as Davidovich's attempts.

Her reverie had to cease, however, when Helen arrived at her side and asked, 'How are things with our Bobby, Mum?'

Sally shrugged. 'Don't know. Just waiting to hear.'

'Do you think it would help if he was told that I'm here?'

Glancing up at the young woman who had just spoken, Sally noted that she was a willowy redhead who oozed a sense of breeding and confidence. But who was she and what was she doing here? But as panic was still overwhelming her, all Sally could ask was, 'And you are?'

The lassie immediately put out her hand to Sally. 'I'm Lois. Bobby and I are an item. But I'm sure he's told you all about us.'

Sensing her mother's disquiet, Helen quickly interjected. 'Lois and Bobby are on the same course at Edinburgh University. Imagine it, before long they will both have LLBs.'

Lois's smile was so warm that it unnerved Sally, and then she said, 'Yes. We will both be solicitors and in time we are aiming to have our own practice.'

'You are?' was all Sally could stutter.

Lois nodded. 'How do you think Hamilton and Stuart sounds?'

Sally was about to answer that she thought it would be better if they called themselves Stuart and Hamilton when the consulting-room door opened.

Proceeding over to Sally with an out-stretched hand, the doctor smiled before saying, 'As you know, your lad had a bad tumble that resulted in him fracturing his right leg, but we have X-rayed it, looked at the problem and we can, when the swelling dies down, reset it. At first he will require a heavy plaster, but after a couple of days we should be able to fit a lighter one and he can go home.'

'Hmm. So everything's fine?' Sally quickly asked.

The doctor inhaled deeply and exhaled before saying, 'Not quite. You see, there is the possibility that your son's damaged leg will be slightly shorter.'

Sally laughed. 'That's alright. You see, he was born with that leg shorter than the other.'

'No. What I mean is your son's right leg will be slightly shorter again, maybe by a quarter of an inch, than it was before the accident.'

Sally sagged against the wall. Shorter could mean his shoe requiring more padding, and would that make his disability evident?

A long half an hour later, Sally, Helen and Lois were allowed in to visit Bobby in his ward bed.

'You okay, son?' was Sally's opening remark.

Bobby nodded and put his hand out to Lois, who lifted it to her mouth and kissed it. 'I'm fine, especially when my three favourite women are at my bedside. Mum, did you introduce yourself to Lois?'

Sally nodded.

'Hope you're pleased, Mum, because Lois and I are...'

'I know: an item.'

Having just arrived home and put the kettle on, Sally was surprised when the doorbell rang continuously. 'Hang on. I'm coming. I'm coming. Do you think I'm a steeple-chaser or something?' she called out as she ran along the hallway.

Once the door was opened, Sally was faced with Margo. 'Oh dear, I forgot I left you with the pub to close. Have you brought the keys?'

Margo fished in her pocket for the keys before handing them to her mother.

'I hope you're not in a hurry, dear?' Sally asked hopefully.

'No. As a matter of fact, I want to talk to you.'

'If it's about Bobby, he'll be fine. And did you know he was courting?'

'Yes, and I told him that he should tell you before someone else did.'

A long, uneasy pause settled on the two women until Margo blurted, 'Mum, a young lassie came into the bar just after you left and she scared me.'

'Scared you? Do you mean she intimidated you? If so, you should have retaliated by threatening her with your Uncle Luke.'

'No, she wasn't trying to get at me. It was you she was after. Said, she did, that you were a traitor and coward.'

Sally began to chuckle. 'Don't be ridiculous,' she spluttered, unable to hide her amusement, 'I was brought up in Leith, and Leith women are faithful and brave until the end.' But when Sally began to grasp that Margo was taking the matter seriously, very seriously, she soberly added, 'Okay. Now what's this lassie's name?'

'Angela.'

'But I don't know an Angela. What's her surname?'

'Yorkston.'

Sally shook her head. 'No, and that doesn't ring a bell either.'

'Pity that, because Mum, her parting shot was she was going to get you to confess what you did to her and more importantly ... take responsibility for your actions.'

'Is the lassie a head-banger or does she think she can frighten me into paying her off? If so, she's in for a disappointment. Did she say when she's coming back?'

'In three days' time.'

Bobby had been kept in the hospital for two days, and when he was due for release, David Stock offered to pick him up in his car and take him home to Sally's home.

When the vehicle came to a halt in Gladstone Place, Sally rushed out to help bring Bobby inside.

On hauling the front door of the car open, Sally was surprised to see Lois sitting in the back, but she did not acknowledge her.

'Right, son,' she began, 'let me get a hold of your crutches so David can help you out.'

'No need, Mum. Lois will get me on to my feet. She was practising it at the hospital before I was discharged.'

'And what will I do?' retorted Sally.

'Do what you're best at and make me

some tea and toast.'

Infuriated, Sally was about to retort, 'Making tea and toast – is that all I'm any good for?' But then she thought the better of it. So smiling sweetly, she turned to Lois and asked, 'And how much sweetening do you require?'

'Sweetening – oh, you mean sugar in my tea – I don't take any.'

'Sweet enough is my Lois,' Bobby said as he started to hobble on his crutches towards the house.

Two hours later, Sally was preparing to leave for the Four Marys when Bobby came into her bedroom. 'Mum, I would like to talk to you. Get some things straight.'

'Look, son, if you're worrying about your leg being shorter – don't. At the most it will only be a quarter of an inch and that will be no problem to Davidovich. Before you know it all your shoes will have been altered and nobody will be able to see the difference.'

'I know that. And, Mum, you worry more about my leg than I do. Short by under half an inch is all that's wrong with me now. And that's nothing.'

Lois had now joined them and had taken up a seat on the bed. 'Now,' she teased, 'I would have to agree with your mother that half an inch can make a big difference.'

Before she could respond, Sally patted her

flaming cheeks. What was this lassie implying? *Surely Bobby and her are not... They just can't be... No, no, sex is a no-go topic in this house.* She knew from working in the pub that the young people of today went on about sex as if the survival of the human race depended on it, but surely her children... Eventually, her mind still in turmoil, she managed to mumble, 'Makes no difference who agrees with me, Lois. My son's welfare is my top priority.'

Lois seemed to ponder before she came back with a torpedo. 'But, Mrs Stuart,' she simpered, 'next year, after Bobby and I get married, you'll be able to spend your time on more worthwhile things than worrying about Bobby's right leg.'

Turning to Bobby expectantly, Sally shrieked, 'Married?'

'Yeah, Mum, just as soon as both of us have graduated we will tie the knot. Mum, I know you will be thrilled for us. Believe me, in my whole life I have never been happier than I am right now.'

As the enormity of what she had done dawned on her, Josie halted packing her suitcase. Soon she would be homeward bound. However, now the euphoria of buying a holiday home had worn off, she had to face the financial reality: a reality that had her screaming inside coupled with a desire to run away. How on earth was she going to cope with Sally's wrath when she told her how reckless she had been?

Sally had always been so good to her; she'd even gifted her half the deposit for her lower-flatted villa in Ryehill Terrace, the house that had quickly become her special wee palace, her very own home where she was mistress and accountable to no one.

Financially, she was sound – or to be precise had been sound – but the second mortgage she now had tied around her neck would change all that. She knew she was crazy to have signed the agreement to purchase. She also knew she would never be able to explain the feeling of exhilaration that had overtaken her when she'd looked at the artist's impression of the flat. Perhaps it was the need to have something of her very own that had driven her. Always she had wanted to belong – to have something that was entirely hers and would be the envy of all.

Anyway, she conceded, *if things get too tough for me there is always Sally to fall back on. In fact, I'll do everything in my power to have Sally take over the responsibility of buying the flat, or at least come in as part-owner.* Having thought out this solution to her problem, she struggled into her swimsuit for one last swim in the warm, exotic waters of the Mediterranean. After all, it was important that she felt rested and relaxed before going home to face the music.

'Sally, are you listening to me?' Rita demanded of Sally, who was away in a world of her own.

'Aye. Aye,' was Sally's dreamy response.

'Well, as your Josie will be back tomorrow, I think you and I should shift ourselves and get the place looking spic and span for her coming back. The state your Margo left it in – didnae even rinse the glasses and wipe ower the tables... Are you sure she's your bairn?'

'Aye. But she takes after her dad. Still needs to be spoon-fed,' was Sally's sarcastic reply.

Before the two women could go on about Margo's shortcomings, a loud, persistent knocking on the door had Rita rushing to open it. 'Och, it's only you, Luke. Now tell me do, have you been promoted to the CID or have you lost your police uniform?'

In answer to Rita's question, Luke nodded and then shook his head. 'Sally,' he began urgently, 'have you seen anything of Irish?'

'No. Is there a problem?'

'Aye. Didn't he get himself in tow with that wee bitch of a lassie again. And didn't she agree to marry him and become, well...'

'But she didn't.'

'Well, she did marry him, but she didn't...

Poor sod had managed to get himself a job on one of the Ben Line ships and did he no leave her most of his pay? But when he got back, well, in addition to being skint... You know how she carries on ... like a bitch in heat, she is.'

'Oh, I hope he doesn't throw himself in the dock again.'

'Wish it would be just a case of dragging him out... Sally, he bought a big gutting knife in Galloway's the ship chandlers yesterday. And see when I asked him why he needed it he said, "To gut with: what else would I do with it?" But after I left him I just knew he meant to rearrange her internal organs with it.'

'But if that's the case then is Irish not a problem for the CID? You're off duty, so why are you concerning yourself?'

'I know Irish is not the brightest shilling in the purse, but I like the guy.'

Before Sally could go on, in came John Thomson and an older man who walked with the aid of a stick. 'I know it's taken a couple of years to get him here, but here he is, Sally: my dad, Jock. And look, Dad, Luke's here too.'

The old gentleman firstly shook Luke's outstretched hand and then he offered to shake Sally's.

Sally became quite emotional when she noticed that as Jock sought her hand he was crying. 'Sorry, hen,' he blurted. 'You see you remind me of ... well, your lovely mother, Peggy Mack.'

'Surely not,' was Sally's quick reply.

'Yeah. She was some lady. Her face, it was the fairest of them all. And she liked nothing better than for the two of us...'

Wishing to hurry things on, Sally asked, 'Would you like a pint of McEwan's Best on the house, Jock?'

'Aye, lass, I would. And I think that offering me hospitality is right civil of you. But then are we not both well bred, and I think you should know...'

Before Jock could finish, in rushed a constable. 'Luke, and you too, John, all hell's broken out at the station. A bairn's gone missing. So they need every man whether he's on duty or not.'

John was the first to react. 'Look, I'll come, but I have to get my dad safely home to Prince Regent Street first.'

Jock and John had just left when Rita said, 'Luke, are you no going to look for Irish? I know a missing bairn is serious, but there'll be plenty there at the station to get the searches started. Please dinnae let the daft laddie doon. You wouldnae want to see him doing time for parting her heid from her shoulders.'

Luke nodded, but before he could leave, Angela entered and minced her way over the bar floor. Immediately she said, 'No need for an introduction, Mrs Stuart, I would have known you anywhere.'

'You would?' Sally exclaimed.

'Yes. To be truthful, you look much older than I thought you would look, but the family resemblance is still there.'

'That might be true. But could I put you right – you are not of my family.'

This statement had a profound effect on Angela. Uncontrollable rage surged within her and as the desire for vengeance was so strong, she couldn't keep herself from raising her hand and slapping Sally hard across the face.

'Why did you do that?' Sally yelped, whilst massaging her stinging face.

Angela, who felt exhilarated by her action, decided to reply by lifting the full pint of beer left by Jock, which she then slowly poured over the top of Sally's head. As the beverage dripped down Sally's face, all that could be heard was Angela's wicked cackle.

Next thing Sally knew was that her forehead and nose had been bounced off the wooden bar and both were bleeding. profusely. Then, without warning, two fingers groped under her face until they found her nostrils, which they then pinched mercilessly together. Waves of blackness and terror were overtaking her and she thought she was about to die. Suffocation looked like being the end of her, but the will to live took over. She would never know where the strength came from, but it did, and she managed to lift up her right high-heeled foot and with a downward thrust she plunged the heel hard into her assailant's ankle. This action either frightened the person or had them judge that killing her was not going to solve anything, so luckily they removed their fingers and Sally breathed freely again.

On hearing the commotion, Rita, who had gone into the kitchen, emerged wielding a large carving knife. 'Now,' she hollered, 'what's going on in here?' Sally's battered and bleeding face was all the answer she required. 'Right now,' she bellowed as she swung the knife, 'let's get this straight. Anybody that's thinking o' starting anything be warned I'll finish it.'

Luke, who had somehow got himself quickly behind the bar, went up to Angela and asked, 'What's your name?'

'Angela Yorkston.'

'Then Angela Yorkston I'm arresting you on the charges of breach of the peace and assault.'

'But,' exclaimed Angela, 'I admit I poured the beer over her and slapped her face, but it was either you or herself who battered her face off the bar. Besides, you should be arresting her for what she has done to me – or hasn't done for me.'

Angela's plea was wasted on Luke, who quickly came round to the front of the bar and began dragging her towards the door. 'Look,' she pleaded, 'you have to listen to my story. Believe me, what happened here tonight is completely out of character for me. I was driven to it.'

'That's what they all say,' Luke replied. 'But tell you what, you can tell me your whole package of woes down at the station. I guarantee, I do, that you'll have my undivided attention for the full two hours before I take up my nightshift duty.'

Once Luke and Angela had left, Rita rushed over to Sally. 'Och, Sally, your bonny face. All cut and bleeding.'

Sally coughed and spat.

'Merciful God, she's knocked out one of your teeth. And the cut on your nose needs stitching, so you'll need to go to the hospital.'

Dishy Dr Falconer was on duty when Sally arrived at the Leith Hospital Casualty Department.

'Hmm,' he hummed. 'Could have been much worse. Fortunately the tooth you've lost was a front overlapping one that should have been removed years ago.'

As the doctor had Sally's mouth wide open so he could inspect for any further damage, Sally could only garble, 'So I'm supposed to feel grateful that I've only been scarred for life instead of dead.'

Iain Falconer laughed. 'You are nowhere near being dead. And as to being defaced for life well, let's have a look.' He then held her cheeks in his hands and twisted them backwards and forwards. 'Take my word for it, in three weeks nobody will ever guess that you've been in the wars.'

'But my tooth won't grow back, will it?'

'That's true. But as I've already said, that tooth should have been extracted a long time ago.' He inhaled before continuing. 'And once your lip, where the tooth crushed into it, heals, you'll see exactly what a blessing in disguise the removal of that tooth has been.'

Sally said no more. So he got on with inserting a couple of stitches into the side of her nose. 'That's you brand new,' Iain teased, helping her off the chair. 'Now, if you just wait, your sister Daisy is coming down to see you.' He added with a cheeky smirk, 'And me too, I hope. Going to the hospital dance with me next week, she is.'

'Oh God, no,' Sally said to herself, 'not another romance that I didn't know about!'

Luke had intended to take Angela to the station to be charged. He knew that was what he was obliged to do. But as soon as they left the Four Marys, Angela had started to unburden herself and tell him her life story.

This meant by the time they reached the Charlotte Street Police Headquarters, he was shaken and shocked. Her story had been so heart-rending that he knew, even if it cost him his job, there was no way he would take her in to be questioned by any of his colleagues.

The dreadful cruelty that had been inflicted on the lassie by one of his own was more than he could bear. He judged that if ever the truth did get out the whole family would be shunned.

What could he do with her then? The only place that he knew where she would be out of danger and the family's secret safe was at Sally's. After all, Sally had lied through her teeth. No way could she convince him that she didn't know all about Angela. She could so easily have ended the lassie's agony and taken her in her arms and told her the truth. But because so much more of the family's dirty washing would then have to be aired in public, Sally had done what she was an expert at – protected herself by remaining silent. This being the case, as he saw it, he decided to go at once to Sally's.

As the dilemma engulfed him, he inhaled deeply before blowing out his lips and hissing inwardly, he spat, 'Yes, to hell with what you want, Sally. You created this mess. You cannot pretend it doesn't exist, and it has to be put right! So here we come.'

David Stock's car was just drawing up at Sally's house in Gladstone Place when Luke and Angela arrived.

Alighting from the vehicle, Sally let out a scream when she saw Angela. 'Luke, you are an insensitive pig. How dare you bring that vandal to my door.'

Luke moved towards Sally and grasped her arm. 'Sally,' he hissed in a hoarse whisper, 'you have to take this lassie in. After all, if anybody knows who she is ... it's holier-than-thou you.' Dragging her arm out of Luke's grasp, Sally was about to retaliate, but Luke continued, 'And before you say another word, say goodbye to goody, goody-two shoes – none other than Chief Inspector Stock.'

Sally shook her head.

'Shake your head all you like, Sally, but if he gets a whiff of what I'm doing he'll report it and I'll be flung out of the force on my ear – he'll have no other option but to hand me in.' Sally looked aghast but Luke ignored her concern and went forcibly on. 'And if he does, you won't be worrying any more about the pong from the sewage works at Seafield. Believe me, a fouler stink will engulf all of us, and no matter how hard we try to wash it off ... the stench will remain.'

Sally was now in a state of confusion. What on earth was Luke going on about?

She knew it was all to do with this strange lassie, Angela, a slip of a woman who had had the temerity to barge into her life and turn it upside down.

Still emotionally frail, Sally began to sob. *Why,* she thought, *is Luke demanding that I send David away? Would it not make more sense for me to keep one ally close by?* Plucking at the front of her coat, she observed Luke again and she noticed that her normally completely-in-control brother was panicking.

Inwardly, she was still reluctant to send David away. After all, was it not true that Luke and herself had never had an easy relationship? But here he was asking – no, begging – for her help, and had he not come to her rescue when Angela assaulted her?

Against her better judgement, she heard herself say, 'Thank you, David. You have been very kind, but it's time you got back home to your wife. She needs you. And don't worry, because Luke and Angela will take care of me.' She weakly smiled to him, but it belied the fact that she was thinking the blow to her face and nose must have rendered her senseless – unable to make a logical decision. That had to be the irrational reason as to why she was inviting two people who really hated her into her home. These people who knew she would have no protection ... not one single ally close by to come to her aid.

The hotel business was successful for Ginny, and she proved very quickly that the large profits were indeed to be made between the sheets. That was why she was always on the lookout for new premises. Someone had told her about an eight-roomed house down in Seaview Terrace in Joppa that was crying out to be developed into a bed and breakfast.

Ginny prided herself in the fact that she was a woman before her time. She was a successful businesswoman who could beat any man any day. Nonetheless, there were things she should have done but hadn't: for instance, she never seemed to find the time to get driving lessons, so she didn't have a driving licence and therefore she didn't own a car.

What she did have was plenty of money to spend on hired vehicles, so the day she decided to inspect the house at Seaview she arrived by taxi.

On arrival at the address, she had asked the driver to drop her off on the grass verge on the other side of the street from the houses so she could view the property she was interested in.

The row of superior houses impressed her. They had obviously been built at a time when it was fashionable to own substantial property close to the beach. Scanning along the edifices, she noted that only two other houses in the long row had been turned into lodging accommodation.

Crossing over the street, she climbed the steps to the house that was for sale and with a flourish she rang the bell.

Half an hour later, Ginny was standing on the doorstep making her departure. 'Are you interested in the house?' the seller asked.

Ginny, being Ginny, had done her research. She knew the middle-aged woman doing the selling was the daughter of the recently deceased owner and she was anxious to get a quick sale so she could return to America, which she now called home.

'For myself – no,' Ginny drawled. 'I like small hotels that I can enlarge. So this is too little for me to develop far enough. But,' she hesitated, 'I do think I know, of someone who this would be a good stepping stone for.'

'You mean you know someone who may be interested in...' The woman abruptly stopped. What she was thinking was 'a broken-down, badly maintained and in much need of repair, shortly to be condemned building'. But, fixing an insincere smile on her face, she continued sweetly to Ginny, 'A house that has so much potential? A place that could be developed and wear the stamp of the personality of the person who buys it.'

Sighing before indicating with her finger,

Ginny pointed out to the sea. At that minute in time the tide had ebbed and the sea was calm and it twinkled like diamonds in the morning sun. 'See there,' she began, 'that magnificent view.' The woman nodded enthusiastically. 'That is the only thing this house has going for it right now.'

'But I thought you said you knew someone who might buy this?'

'I do. But ... let's say ... you would have to become more realistic about the asking price.'

Morning hadn't come too soon for Sally. She wanted to believe that Angela was a Walter Mitty character, but what she said about her having been born to a young teenager who then left her in the orphanage fitted in with Josie having disappeared when she was just fifteen. What also became more believable with the dawn was how Angela's grandmother in America had found out that she existed and then she'd come over, and taken on the establishment and won – won the right to adopt her own granddaughter, who she had cared for ever since.

There were other things that were perplexing Sally. One was why had Josie not sought her help? For God's sake, she was only fifteen and pregnant to a GI who had been sent to France, which meant she had been left all alone to face the condemnation that was poured onto all unwed mothers to be. Hadn't she trusted Sally enough to ask for understanding? Why, hadn't she known that Sally loved her dearly and would have forgiven her anything? Sally stopped in her deliberations. *Why*, she scolded herself, *would Josie require my forgiveness? The only person in this sorry affair that she should beg absolution from is Angela.*

The other matter that was of great concern was that when Mrs Yorkston had contacted her and offered her assistance, even – if Angela was to be believed – to take her to America and care for her and Angela, why hadn't Josie taken up this generous offer? Sally had thought up till now that Josie, who lived in a land of make-believe, would just have loved to have been offered the chance of emigration to America. Why hadn't she grabbed the chance to live the American dream? Angela's grandmother appeared to be a warm and loving woman. Was that not always what Sally and her siblings had yearned for: a supportive, affectionate mother figure?

Thinking of a mother figure caused Sally to draw up. She smiled. *Now wasn't that just fortuitous of me to have persuaded Flora to have a telephone installed.* Flora had been reluctant to give the contraption houseroom and took delight in saying, 'Don't be daft, Sally. You know fine there's a call box just five minutes down the road that I can use if there's an emergency.' What she didn't add but thought was, *Besides, I sleep a lot easier when I'm not privy to every little crisis that happens down in Leith – especially if my darling Bobby sneezes twice.* Nonetheless, after much persuasion she had relented and the telephone, just for use in *real* emergencies, was installed.

After dialling Flora's number, Sally had to wait for what seemed an eternity before she answered. 'Hello. Is there a fire or something?' Flora huffed. 'Surely you know hens have to be fed and eggs collected?'

'Flora, it's Sally.'

'Of course I knew it was you, Sally. Nobody else ever rings this abomination's bell.'

Ignoring the rant that was always Flora's opening remarks, Sally, without enquiring as to Flora's well-being, said, 'Flora, now I want you to cast your mind back.'

'To where?'

'Look, it's just, do you remember when you went to Blackpool to see the lights and you came back with Josie?'

'Hardly likely to forget that happy day, am I?' Flora shouted – not through frustration this time but because she thought she had to heighten her voice so Sally could hear her in Edinburgh.

'Right, now what I want is for you to concentrate hard and try and recall did Josie say anything about a baby or a GI or America?'

A long pause followed.

'Flora, Flora, are you still there? What I am asking is...'

'I know what you're asking and I'm trying to remember, but it's such a long time ago. Blast this getting old. The only thing going for it is you get a pension. Now, what did Josie say that day?' There followed a long hesitation during which Flora hummed and hawed. Eventually she drawled, 'No, Josie never mentioned nothing about a baby or an American GI. Though I think if she'd come across the GI she would have been pleased, very pleased... Just said, she did, that she had to run away because someone we all knew was trying to get her to do things that no lassie should do unless she's been churched.'

Sally sighed. Flora was getting old, and every week now when she rang her there were always problems. If it wasn't that she didn't have her distance glasses on so she couldn't see to hear Sally then it was her hearing itself that was bad. The hearing had the habit of getting really bad if Sally ever had reason to criticise any of the children – especially Bobby.

'Okay, Flora, you get back to the hens. And don't you concern yourself about not knowing about what Josie forgot to tell us when you found her. When I've caught up with her and got the whole story, I'll ring you.'

Sally hung up, but not in time not to hear Flora scream, 'Is there a story here that I should know about? Sally, Sally, you tell me now. Knowing Josie I bet it's juicy and...'

Before Sally could go any further with her enquiries, the doorbell rang. Thinking that Luke had made good progress in bringing Josie home from Glasgow Airport, she skipped along the corridor.

'Gosh that was quick,' she said, yanking the door open.

'Clairvoyant are you now,' Ginny quipped as she brushed past Sally and proceeded towards the living room.

'Thought you were Luke,' Sally explained when she caught up with Ginny.

'Don't tell me that the two of you are being civil to each other? Now that is a turn-up for the books.'

'He is just away to Glasgow to pick up Josie. She's been on holiday in Menorca.'

'But why would he bring her here? She has a home of her own now.'

'Just a wee family problem we have to get straightened out.'

'And I hope by the look of your face it will not end up in any more blows.'

Fingering her swollen nose and bruised cheek, Sally replied, 'This mess. Och, you know how it's a hazard of the trade. But you should see the other guy – came off worse, he did.'

'Hmm,' observed Ginny, who wasn't convinced by Sally's excuse. 'Now what I'm here for is I've got this great idea.'

Sally groaned. Ginny, she knew, did get good ideas, but today, with the Angela affair to be straightened out, Sally could do without any further proposals for consideration.

Ignoring Sally's reluctance, Ginny sallied on. 'Now Sally, just listen. I've just been to see this wonderful house in Joppa.' She paused. 'Okay, it's not wonderful just now, but it will be once you've spent time and money on it. Honestly, Sally, it has so much potential and it's a snip. Or it will be once you've beaten the greedy woman – American she is – down.'

'But I have a nice home here. I love it. Why would I want to move?'

'Because, my dear Sally, as I'm always pointing out to you, it's easier to make your money between the sheets than it is in a bar in Leith – where you are in danger of having your face rearranged.'

Sally shrugged.

Ginny continued, 'Believe me, this house is just crying out to be developed into a bed and breakfast, and it could also be your stepping stone to starting up your own hotel empire.'

Sally knew she should argue, but she just didn't have the energy or motivation to do so. Ginny was a dear friend and she knew she had her best interests at heart. It was true Sally could have more time to herself if she hadn't the two bars to supervise, but she liked working in the trade. Not wishing to hurt or alienate Ginny, she found herself saying, 'Ginny, I promise you that I will look at the house. Leave the details, but today I just have to get a family problem straightened out.'

Ginny, who was one never to let an opportunity pass by, responded, 'And while you're about it, get rid of PC 49. He has an ailing wife.' Sally made to interrupt, but Ginny silenced her with a wave of her hand, 'And yes, I know, because I know you, it's platonic, but since they introduced the birth control pill who ever believes any relationship is not sexual?'

'The problem I'm dealing with has nothing to do with David. It's...'

The door opened and a tousled, half-slept Angela, carrying a teddy bear, sauntered in.

'Oh. Now aren't you the dark horse? Here was me thinking I would put you on track to becoming a hotel owner and here you have already started by taking in paying guests.'

'I'm not a visitor,' an indignant Angela said defensively. 'Am I, Aunt Sally?'

Sally shrugged and waved her hands. 'No. Ginny, this here is Angela. She's...' Sally just didn't know what to say, because until Josie confirmed that she had had a child, nobody could be positively sure she had.

'Josephine's daughter,' Angela informed her.

Not sure if she had heard right, Ginny exclaimed, 'Are you claiming that Josie, when she was a scatterbrain, gave birth to you?'

Angela nodded.

'And you are also asking me to believe that she scooted off on holiday and left you behind?'

'No. She doesn't know that I've managed to track her down. It will be as big a surprise to her as it was to you when she comes in and finds me here.'

Lifting her handbag, Ginny began to make for the door. 'Sally, I think as you appear to have your hands full I'll take off for now, but...' She paused whilst pulling on her gloves, '...don't forget the house in Seaview. Terrace, Joppa. You really must consider it – especially now you have relatives popping out of all sorts of holes in the woodwork.'

Two hours passed before Luke came back into Sally's.

'Where's Josie?'

'Look Sally, you know how hazardous that car trip from Glasgow Airport is. That A8 is a death trap ... and okay they're upgrading it bit by bit ... but as I didn't want to end up in bits, I didn't mention Angela to Josie.'

Luke turned to Angela. 'Unpredictable

your mother is when she gets a shock. Don't know how she'll react. After all, did you not demonstrate last night how volatility runs in the family? Besides... All Josie could do was babble on about how wonderful Menorca was and – wait for it, Sally – how she might be becoming the owner of a flat there!'

The information about Josie thinking about buying a holiday home went straight over Sally's head. 'But I told you,' she protested, 'to tell her and get the initial shock over for her.'

'Look, Mrs Righteousness, if you're so keen on having that done and since I've just dropped our Josie off at her house why don't I drive you and Angela up there and the two of you can break the good news to her.'

Luke had just dropped Sally and Angela off at Josie's door when Angela grabbed Sally's arm. 'Aunt Sally,' she whimpered, 'what if she still doesn't want to know me?'

Sally took a deep intake of breath and exhaled it slowly before responding, 'The only way we'll find that out and why she did what she did is to ring this bell.'

On opening the door and finding Sally and Angela standing there, Josie became wary. She could tell from Sally's demeanour that all was not well. Sensing that somehow Sally had found out she had signed up to buy a flat and thinking that Angela was probably the British agent, she gulped, stood aside and allowed them to enter.

Once they had all got seated, Josie began. 'Please don't be angry. I can explain. And if we all work together, we will be able to sort everything out.'

Sally gasped. 'For heaven's sake, Josie, I know you can be feckless at times, but how do you reckon that by sitting down and talking about it you can sort everything out? You just can't. This lassie here is your child, Angela!'

Dumbfounded, Josie started to stutter, 'But I thought she was the British mortgage advisor?'

'No, she bloody well is not,' Sally exploded. 'She is, in case you have gone deaf and didn't hear me, the daughter you abandoned in a soulless orphanage in 1945!'

Josie slipped off her seat. Cries like those of a wounded animal escaped her. With her bare hands she thumped on the floor. Still whimpering, she slowly began to crawl towards Angela, but Angela turned away from her. All her life she had wanted to face her mother. Have her mother put out her arms to her. But this whimpering, cringing creature was not the kind of mother she had ever envisaged her mother to be. She had been hard enough to desert her, hard enough to ignore the pleas of her grandmother, and here she was cowed, frightened, grovelling.

The cries of Josie were so distressing that Sally dropped down beside her and lifted her up in her arms. 'Sally,' she pleaded as Sally rocked her from side to side, 'this young woman cannot be my little girl. She'll not be fully grown yet.' She paused and through her tears she glanced at Angela. 'Every night I dream of her. I know it's not her because, oh, Sally, dreams never come true.'

'It is her, and what you have got to do is pull yourself together and tell us why you acted in the way you did.' Looking towards Angela, Sally softly added, 'This lassie here, your very own child you gave birth to, deserves to know the truth.'

Unable to control her anguish, Josie trembled and sobbed. 'I met,' she began falteringly, 'fair-haired, deep blue-eyed Roy Yorkston at a dance in a café on Princes Street.' Josie now seemed to go into a story-line that she had told herself over and over again and again. 'He wasn't tall, but was tall enough for me. And his smile ... it would have melted the iceberg that hit the *Titanic*, and see the first time he called me "babe" in his American drawl my legs felt like jelly. I'd never been in love like this before. He was my Rhett Butler and I was his Scarlett. From the moment we kissed we knew we loved each other and were destined to love each other forever. Still love him, and only him, I do.'

A strange, eerie silence filled the room. It was as if the ghost of Roy had come in and joined them. After a while, Josie felt she had to put some things right and suddenly the stillness of the room was broken by her blurting, 'Now don't run away with the idea we were doing ... well, you know what. No, not even when he showered me with nylons, chocolate and chewing gum. Please believe we'd been going out at least three months before we... Anyway I found out I was having...' She faltered before adding, '...his child, but he was on embarkation leave, so he promised to come back and make it alright for me – and I now know he would have, but when you get killed you just don't seem to be able to keep your promises.'

Sally smiled. This story was all too typical of Josie – just like an American film.

'Anyway, Sally,' Josie went on, 'you know what like Mum was. She would have wanted me to abort ... our baby so I decided to run away to Morecambe, where I gave birth to her in an unmarried mothers' home there. They wanted me to hold her, look at her, but you see I thought that Roy had deserted me. How could I look after and provide for a baby? And I didn't want to end up with people saying I was like Mum. I knew if I had ever looked at her, I would never ever have been able to leave the home without her.'

Angela huffed.

'For Christ's sake, I'd only turned sixteen. I was frightened ... alone ... with nobody to turn to!'

'You're a blasted liar,' Angela spat. 'My grandmother wrote to you, begged you to go to her. She wanted nothing more than to be your friend, to look after us, and you didn't even have the decency to reply.'

Josie was crying uncontrollably now. 'And do you know when I got all those letters?'

Angela and Sally both shook their heads.

'When my mother died... Tied up in red ribbon they were.' Josie looked to Sally. 'Please tell me you remember the bundle of letters addressed to me that were in her things?'

Sally nodded. She knew her mother was cruel, but what had been done to Josie by keeping the letters from her was as bad as having Peter birched. She had ruined Josie's life. But why? Time ticked slowly by but eventually Sally said, 'Please, Josie, don't tell me that the old, twisted witch kept your letters from you?'

Josie nodded and began pounding the floor again. 'She did. She did. She did. So you see, Angela, it was 1955 that I got your grandmother's letters. You were nine years old going on ten. So how could I come into your life then?'

'Are you saying that your very own mother

hid those letters from you?'

'Mother?' Sally loudly exclaimed. 'Oh Angela, don't give her a title she has no right to. She was a fiend. How she got like that will forever be a mystery to me.'

Sally began to drag Josie to her feet, but before letting go of her, she held her close and, brushing her lips over her hair, she acknowledged that Josie had known so much turmoil and so much unhappiness. No wonder she had never really allowed any relationship to develop.

Glancing at Angela, she remembered her own miserable childhood when all she ever wanted was a loving mother. Feelings of anger, sadness and betrayal engulfed and confused her before, thankfully, forgiving comprehension dawned. 'Look,' she said slowly and softly to Angela, 'I don't want you to worry about last night when you assaulted me and knocked my tooth out. I now understand how frustrated you must have felt. And you did believe I was your mother. So I forgive you.'

'Look, I admit I slapped your face and poured a pint of beer over your head, but I did *not* bang your head down on the bar.'

Sally looked bewildered. Her head had been bounced off the bar and someone had then pinched in her nostrils until, through lack of oxygen, she had experienced the sensation of blacking out. *But*, she pondered, *if*

Angela is telling the truth then who was it that wanted to hurt me? Reluctantly she had to accept that there was no mileage for Angela in lying. She had confessed that she had slapped her and poured the beer over her. So why would she not be prepared to own up to the head-banging? But who else was there? Sally's blood began to run cold. Luke's words when their mother had died echoed in her head. 'No matter how long it takes, I'll get vengeance for my mother. You mark my words that I will.' *Oh no*, she cried inwardly, *Luke, Luke. Surely after all we've been through as a family... Can't you accept that Mum had her shortcomings...? So why would you wish to still have me pay, and for what?*

The noise of sobbing broke into Sally's reverie. While she had been thinking, she had moved about the room and she was now standing with her back to the window. The pitiful wails were coming from Josie, who was seated on the floor with her arms about Angela's legs. 'Please, please,' Sally heard Josie beg, 'since you were born I have ached for you. Could you...' racking sobs interrupted the flow, '...not let me be friends with you?'

Angela, while trying desperately to extricate herself from Josie's grasp, was also weeping, albeit quietly.

Going over to her sister and her niece, Sally lifted Josie up. Firstly she brushed the tears from Josie's cheeks and then she stroked her hair. 'Don't either of you,' she mumbled, 'go too fast in accepting or rejecting each other. A relationship between the two of you is important. It cannot be forged quickly. Take your time. Build bridges. And eventually something may...' Sally stopped, as Angela had stood up and had started buttoning up her coat. 'Why did you really come here, Angela, if not to trace your mother?' she asked softly.

'Next year I'm getting married and I'm so afraid that when I have children that I won't love them ... or not love them enough. So I asked my grandmother to tell me all she knew about my mother. You see, she always told me that my mother couldn't come to America because there were important things that kept her here. It was also my grandmother who suggested I come here and try and make some sense of why my mother rejected me.'

A wail escaped from Josie. 'No. No. I didn't reject you. I wanted you to have some sort of life. I didn't want you labelled ... *bastard*. Do you know how difficult it was for me to walk away?'

'No. But you did,' was Angela's caustic reply.

'Look. I've said my piece,' Sally interjected. 'Let's not say nothing can be salvaged. Give it time. For a start, I have a lot on my plate right now plus I don't want my doting public to see my face while it looks like I lost a prize fight.' Sally glanced up at the clock before continuing. 'So that means in two hours' time the Four Marys will require to be opened up by you, Josie. So get yourself freshened up and get down there. Now to you, Angela, I don't carry passengers; therefore, you can make yourself useful by working with your mother tonight.' Angela visibly squirmed. 'But, okay, at bedtime you can sleep at my house. Tomorrow, well ... like the Forth Rail Bridge ... it will take time, a long time, to build a secure structure.' To herself, Sally added, *And perhaps like the Tay Rail Bridge, no matter how hard you try you won't be able to stop yourselves from toppling into the water.*

Luke had just taken up the back shift duty of the Shore beat when John Thomson, who had just gone off duty, stuck his head back through the police box door. 'Nearly forgot the lad you befriended...'

'Now which one would that be?' queried Luke, who gave succour to so many that he couldn't keep track of them all.

'The lad you nicknamed Irish.'

'Oh, him. But he's at sea just now,' Luke, who already knew there were problems with Irish, lied

'Was, and when he got back hadn't his

bride made a mug of him again. According to the barmaid in the Ship Inn, he went berserk and threatened to kill her. Now both of them are missing and we've to keep an eye out for them. Or, if you've got any sense, run the other way if you see them coming.'

'Bye,' was all Luke replied, hoping that he would find Irish before it was too late.

'But here, before I go, my dad is still desperate to have a talk to you about your mother – wants to put some things right about her. Honestly, he just goes on and on about it. You do know he's got the old folks' trouble – dementia?'

Luke nodded.

John continued, 'Cannae remember what he had for breakfast, but he's spot on about things in the past. When would you be free?'

The last thing Luke wished for was to get involved in any more past family matters, especially as, in his opinion, they should now be forgotten. And as to his mother... It was true he had adored her and could never see any wrong in her, but having been told by Sally about what she, his lovely mother, had done with Josie's letters and then her reiterating the birching of Peter, he was starting to have doubts. But here was John's father Jock Thomson wanting to tell him tales about his mother. Was it possible that old Jock would be able to tell him stories that would restore his faith in his beloved mum? Thinking that was a possibility, he replied, 'Sure. I'll be weekend off next week so how about I meet him in the Four Marys on the Saturday afternoon?'

'That's just great, Luke. And get your sisters to come along too. I think what he has to say about your mother they all should hear.'

Five minutes later, Luke was still reading the big summation book when he was summoned to the door. 'Not something else you forgot to tell me, John?' he joked when he opened the door to find his colleague standing there.

'Oh my God, Luke, I've just noticed a body floating in the water, and as you are a better swimmer than I am I thought...'

'Look, John, is the body screaming to be saved?'

'No. I think it is beyond saving.'

'Then there would be no point to me jumping in. Let's get a boat and fish it out.'

One of the things that Leith dockers were good at was leaving their posts to attend to emergencies. Sometimes the predicament was as simple as a case of twelve-year-old malt whisky on its way to Venezuela finding itself lost and in need of some benefactors to rescue it and keep it in Scotland. Today the cry had gone up that there was a body in the water.

Immediately eight stout souls were coming

to the rescue. Firstly they launched the small rowing craft and two mates set sail in her whilst the other six shouted instructions from the pier.

By the time John and Luke arrived to join in the recovery of the body, it had been hauled on board.

'Man or woman?' Luke, who was praying that it would not be Irish, shouted down to the men in the boat.

'Woman,' replied the oarsman. 'And I think she must have been pushed in.'

'What makes you say that?'

'Just that her eyes are bulging and her scarf looks as if it's so tightly tied around her neck that it's choked her.' The man hesitated. He was enjoying his moment of fame. 'Soooo,' he half sang as he goaded Luke and John, 'I'm not a flat foot, but I'll bet my week's wages that she couldn't have jumped in.'

John turned to Luke and under his breath he observed, 'All we bloody need right now is Sherlock Holmes down there.'

'I'm just so glad it's not Irish that I don't care who solves her demise.'

Luke and John were now helping to drag the body up from the water. 'I think you might care, Luke. Can't be certain, but is she not Irish's wife?'

Half an hour later, two duty detectives attached to 'D' Division arrived. 'Any ideas on what happened here?' the younger of the two enquired of Luke.

The older man drew his assistant aside. 'Look, son, we are the detectives. We work out what has happened and we do not, and never will, ask uniform to make a guess. Uniform are in uniform because they do not think. They have a manual and they do everything by the book.'

'Funny, John,' Luke began, 'I was just about to say to the rookie that he shouldn't pay too much attention to his buddy, because it's the like of him that keeps the dichotomy between the uniform and plain clothes going. But do you think they would know how to spell "dichotomy", never mind understand it.'

John, laughing uproariously, went out of his way to stamp his feet before saying, 'You're right, Luke, so I'm going off duty now, and you would be best to go back to the box and read the book and see if it says anything in there about how to deal with unfeeling, ill-mannered, incompetent bastards.'

Luke nodded, and the two detectives were left to deal with the suspicious death of Marie without the help of uniform.

Going to look at the house in Seaview Terrace was a welcome distraction from family problems for Sally.

For one thing, it was a beautiful night and

the sunset lit up the blue sea in hues of red, orange and yellow. She was completely enchanted, and the thought of owning a house where she could look out on such splendour any time she felt like it filled her with anticipation.

She was just about to climb the five steps up to the front door when it was opened by a middle-aged woman.

'Are you the friend of the lady who called here this morning?'

'Could be,' was Sally's chirpy reply.

Sally was expecting to be invited into the house, but the woman just stood on the doorstep. 'Would you look at that view? On a night like this you can accept that the Spanish sailors sailing up the Forth called this place Portobello. Means "beautiful port", Portobello does.'

Sally nodded. 'And it certainly is. But I have limited time to spare, so could you allow me to view the house?'

'But of course,' responded the woman, opening up the door further. 'But you know I reside in Dakota now, and I didn't know how much I'd missed this view until I came back last month.'

Sally had to admit that Ginny had been right when she had said don't look at all the things that need attention – look at the potential. That was fine for Ginny, who was wealthy and could afford to pour limitless amounts of money into upgrading a building. Sally admitted to herself that she wasn't poor, but she just couldn't see how she could afford to take this house on right now. In addition to getting Helen and Bobby through college there was the mortgage on Gladstone Place, and there was also a financial problem that Josie wanted to speak to her about.

Much to the chagrin of the woman who was selling the house, Sally decided to leave without being very enthusiastic about the property. 'You wish to come back?' the woman asked.

'No ... well ... not really. It could be made into a beautiful house, but I just don't have the time or resources to spend on it just now.'

'I am willing to negotiate.'

Sally thought, *I bet you are. Even although the view from the front of the house over to Fife is spellbinding, you still can't wait to get back to Black Hills.*

Luke was halfway through his shift when he was passing the Carriers Rest pub. He happened to look in and there as bold as brass was Irish, downing a pint of Guinness.

Going over to Irish, he tapped him on the shoulder. 'What's the game?' Luke asked.

'Just having a farewell pint, is there a law against that?'

'No. But what about your Marie?'

'Finished with her and Leith, just like you said I should. Going back to dear old Donegal, I am. But here, pal of mine, how about having a drink with me?'

Luke took Irish by the arm, pulled him away from the bar and pushed him down on a chair at a table. 'What did you do that for?' Irish slurred as he began to get up and make his way back to the bar.

'Sit,' Luke hissed. 'Now you're in big trouble. Marie has just been fished out of the estuary.'

'Did she jump in?'

'No, she didn't. And since you've been telling the entire world and his brother that you were going to do her in, you are a suspect.'

'No. No. I'd never have done her any real harm.' He now began to cry profusely and thump the table. 'I loved her. I married her, but when I discovered she was being run by Stan Roper I knew she was lost ... to ... me.'

'Stan Roper?' Luke exclaimed. 'But he's a right villain. Has his finger in anything that's illegal. He even runs half a dozen pros that are right hard-cases – including, might I add, the boss woman, big Jessie Scott.'

Irish, still trying to pull himself together, just nodded. 'Jessie was livid when Stan took on Marie on better terms than she has. I think,' he sniffed, 'she saw Marie as a threat.'

Luke visibly relaxed. Maybe he had been too quick to come to the conclusion that Irish had done for Marie. He liked Irish, and okay they had done away with hanging, but Irish was an inoffensive, gullible sort of guy, so how would he have survived in prison? Because Luke liked him he wanted to help him, but he was also a police officer and he must do what was right. 'Look, Irish,' he said, taking out his handkerchief and using it to wipe Irish's face and nose, 'the detectives who're investigating your wife, Marie's, death will be needing to take a statement from you. So how about I take you along to the station now and you can give it and then get on with your life – preferably away from my patch.'

Irish nodded. 'Mind you, I'll never love anyone the way I loved... Oh Luke, I was crazy about her. She was ... so lovely. Used to call me her sweet Irish potato... Is that right, she'd been pushed into the water like a bag of rubbish?' Irish's sobs were now uncontrollable.

Luke nodded. Mopping Irish's face again, he then pulled him up on his feet. 'Now come on, pal, the station is only five minutes away.'

Sally had never thought of herself as an artist. However, when she got back from viewing the house in Joppa she had got out her box of Max Factor make-up and started work on her face. When she had finished the touch-up job, she had to admit that unless you looked at her face in full daylight you wouldn't know she had been attacked. She shivered when she thought of the assault. Who had done it? After listening to Angela's tale of her birth and desertion, she could understand why the lassie was so angry and why she would wish to lash out. However, Angela admitted flinging the beer over her but vehemently denied being responsible for the damage to her face.

Having decided that she was presentable enough to go into her bars, she decided that she would do a check on them both. Firstly she would call in on the Royal Stuart and see Nancy, who would no doubt have a few words of wisdom for her, then she would go by taxi to the Four Marys. She shuddered again when she thought of having to sit down with Josie and discuss what financial mess she had got herself into in Menorca.

The taxi she had summoned was chugging on the street when she opened the door, and she was just about to jump in when a voice called, 'Sally, Sally.' Turning, Sally was dismayed to see Maggie running towards her.

'I'm sorry, I'm just on my way to check the bars. Is there something you want?' Sally said in a voice as cold as ice.

Turning to face the women, the driver pointedly said, 'Look, Mrs Stuart, I know you have a contract with me but I do have to pick up other customers so can you get a move on?'

Tutting, Sally replied, 'I'm being as quick as I can. But I have to deal with this lady first.'

'Eh, eh,' stuttered Maggie. 'I don't mean to keep you back. Maybe it would be best if I came back another time.'

The last thing Sally wished was for Maggie to come back later. *Better*, she thought, *to get whatever she wants to say over and done with*. 'No, just jump in beside me, Maggie. After all, I'm going to the Royal Stuart and that's just a stone's throw from where your house is. Right, Tom, let's get going.

'Well, Maggie, you have my undivided attention, so what's your problem?'

'As you can see,' Maggie began falteringly, 'I've been discharged.'

Sally nodded.

'Said they thought I was no longer a danger.'

That right? was Sally's silent response to herself. *Well, maybe not to yourself but what about the rest of us?*

Ignoring Sally's lack of audible reply, Maggie continued, 'You see, I wonder if there was ... by any chance ... you could help me to find work. Lost my job in the store; and now I've been in the Royal Edinburgh everybody thinks I'm some sort of nutcase, so no one will employ me.'

This statement caught Sally off guard. She had not expected Maggie to ask her to give her employment. And what if she did offer her a job? What work could she do? She was only trained to slice bacon, pat butter and sell cornflakes: none of these skills were useful in a bar. Besides, the people she did employ, Josie, Rita and Nancy, wouldn't make Maggie's life easy and that would mean Sally's happy ships might run aground.

They had now reached the Royal Stuart, and as they alighted from the taxi Sally called back, 'Tom, I'll only be here for an hour, so can you pick me up then and take me down to the Four Marys?'

'Nae bother,' he responded and drove off like a bat out of hell.

Forgetting that she was going to shield Maggie from the spite Sally knew would be forthcoming from Nancy, she flounced into the bar with Maggie taking up the rear.

You couldn't say Nancy was surprised when she saw Maggie, but you couldn't mistake the hostility that emanated from her.

'Heard you got a bump on the head last night, but they never said it had rendered you senseless.'

'I'm not.'

'In that case, can you tell me why you have brought that into my bar?' Nancy spat as she eyed Maggie up. 'Now, Sally, you and me have a good relationship, but don't play on it.'

'What do you mean?'

'It's all round Easter Road that she's been looking for a job, but no one wants her. So if you think you can palm her off on me you've got another think coming.'

Nancy's attitude put Sally's back up. Nancy and she had always worked in harmony, and any suggestions Sally made Nancy was always pleased to comply with. But today she was taking her on, and why?

'Are you sure that nobody will have Maggie?'

'Aye,' was Nancy's quick reply, 'She even offered to scrub the floors in the undertakers, but he didn't want to take the chance of her running off with someone's dead husband.'

'Nancy,' Sally began in a warning tone, but she stopped as she saw Maggie was retreating towards the door. 'Maggie, hold on. You knew I couldn't employ you in any of my bars. The women who run them are loyal to me – they are true friends. But tell you what, come and see me in about six weeks. I may have a wee cleaning job for you.'

Maggie, tears brimming over, nodded. 'I knew you would help me if you could. I've been such a fool.'

'Join the club,' Nancy and Sally replied in unison.

Tom had just dropped Sally off at the Four Marys when she became aware of an uneasy atmosphere that seemed to be shrouding the Shore.

She acknowledged it wasn't just the forlorn mist that was swathing the streets and lamplights. It was something else. Something was missing. No singing, no laughter, no high spirits – just hushed whisperings and the mournful warnings of the foghorns.

On entering the public house, she became aware that Josie was behind the bar and Angela was out on the floor collecting glasses. The bar was as busy as it always was when it was nearing closing time. Then people would order up two and three rounds to keep their high spirits well oiled. But not tonight – they all appeared to be nursing one solitary drink.

'Been a death or something?' Sally whispered to Josie.

'Aye. Marie. Irish's wife.'

'Oh no,' exclaimed Sally. 'See, the trade these lassies follow is just so full of danger and pitfalls. Cannae be anything else when they're prepared to go and accommodate the highest bidder – and most of them are weirdoes, Josie.'

'That's no the worst of it,' said Josie.

'No.'

'Our Luke persuaded Irish to go to the station and give a statement. Right mistake that was, because as usual the CID were

276

thinking it was a right waste of their expertise to fully investigate the death of a prostitute, so they charged Irish.'

'But surely, Josie, Luke explained...'

'He tried to. But the CID treat uniform just like the pros.'

'He must be devastated.'

'He is. He's even threatening to leave Leith and transfer to Hong Kong.'

'Hong Kong – that's a bit too far away. Talking of far away, did you not say you wanted to speak to me about a faraway holiday home? Though what's wrong with a chalet in Kinghorn I'll never know.'

Josie blushed. 'Now,' she began as she wiped over the bar, 'it is the chance of a lifetime. Oh Sally, just wait until you've seen Santo Tomas. Honestly, you'll be congratulating me on getting such a bargain. Imagine it: our own wee flat in paradise.'

'Paradise? And how much is paradise costing these days?' came Sally's caustic response.

Josie clucked and shrugged before spluttering, 'A mere ... five thousand!'

'Five blinking thousand?' Sally shouted so loudly that she disturbed the mournful clients. 'You talk about money as if it was peanuts. Are you mad or something?'

Josie shook her head and started to back towards the far wall of the bar.

'Here was me thinking that if I put

Gladstone Place up for sale...'

'You wouldn't need to put your house up for sale to buy the flat in Menorca. The bank will lend you the money. You're in good standing with them.'

'I wasn't going to sell my house to accommodate your flight from blooming reality; I was going to sell it so I could buy a large house in Joppa.'

'But why? Gladstone Place is bigger than your needs,' stated Josie, looking about for someone to agree with her. 'We all work hard, and I think it's only right we have a wee bolt-hole to run to when we need to refresh ourselves.'

'That right? Well, let me tell you, I think all the bolts and screws in your head have come undone and it's high time you got them screwed back into place.'

'Auntie Sally, you are upsetting yourself, so why don't you sit down and I'll fix you a nice cup of tea,' Angela suggested.

'Tea! A flight to Menorca to sort out this mess is what I need, and first thing tomorrow morning you'll find me at the airport.'

After being charged at Leith Police Station, Irish had been taken to the cells at the High Street in Edinburgh. He was to remain there overnight until his preliminary appearance at the High Court the following morning. After that appearance, he would be remanded in Saughton Prison.

Luke was desperate to speak to Irish. He needed to hear from Irish himself what had led to him being charged. He had been apprised of the situation by Holmes and Watson, as the two detectives were known, but somehow he felt it was all too rushed and didn't ring quite true.

Against his better judgement, Luke decided to visit Irish in the cells at the High Street. He knew the officer who was on turnkey duties, whereas if he waited until Irish was taken to Saughton he would not be able to persuade anyone there to allow him access to a prisoner on remand.

Dougal the duty turnkey, huffed and puffed when Luke suggested that he give him just five minutes with Irish. Dougal and Luke had been friends for a few years, so Dougal was easily persuaded by Luke to bend the rules. And, of course, the promise of a bottle of twelve-year-old double malt that had got lost in the docks and was seeking a new home sealed the deal.

When Luke was admitted to Irish's cell, he was appalled at the sight of his friend. He was dirty, unshaven and looked as if he had somehow been in a sparring match where he had come off second best.

'Fine mess you got me into, Luke,' was Irish's opening remark.

'I'm sorry. I didn't know they were already

looking for you and that they had corroborating evidence.'

'What corroborating evidence?'

Luke shrugged.

'What they have,' Irish continued, 'is a sworn statement from Jessie Scott, corroborated by wee Jenny Geddes, who's shit scared of her and Stan Roper. Threatening her, they are, and really putting the frighteners on her.'

'Did you remember to tell them about Marie throwing in her lot with Stan?'

''Course I did. But they weren't interested. They were only keen in fitting me up and thanks to you they did. Now get out of here. I never want to see your stupid bloody face again.'

'Maybe you don't. But I'll be leaving soon, or I hope I will, but I promise you I won't be on any aeroplane until I have got you out of here.'

'Then you'll no be going anywhere.'

Why Sally had come on this trip on her own she didn't know. No one had told her about the turbulence the plane might meet. Never before had she experienced her stomach floating in her mouth and then wishing to empty itself at will. And if that wasn't bad enough, the nun sitting next to her had taken out her rosary beads and begun praying.

Half an hour later when the craft touched down on the runway, the blood-curdling screeching of the brakes sent waves of sheer terror through her. 'Blast Josie,' she shouted out aloud as her nails dug into the armrests.

All she was here for was to get hold of the lassie who had sold Josie the flat and get her to tear the agreement up. She readily accepted that a fine would be imposed for the breaking of the contract. She could live with the loss of a hundred pounds; what she couldn't live with was tying a five-thousand-pound mortgage around her neck, especially when she had other plans.

Hailing taxis she was good at, and within half an hour she was at the resort of Santo Tomas and was being dropped off at the estate agents' office. 'Where are all the staff? It's just gone two o'clock,' she observed to the driver.

The driver, who didn't have much English, had managed to work out that Sally wished to see the estate agent. Hunching his shoulders, he went on to say, 'Siesta time, lady. They be back six o'clock.' He then saluted and drove off.

Sally exhaled by puffing out her lips. What was she going to do for four hours? Nothing but finding the hotel, and having a long, cooling drink and a paddle in the sea.

The Fanta orange drink was so refreshing she had two. Sitting on the hotel balcony, she could see the deep blue sparkling sea and it seemed to beckon to her.

On leaving the bar, she sauntered down to the beach, where she removed her shoes, and as she strolled she allowed the warm sand to massage her feet. Before she knew it she had begun to paddle through the warm, inviting water. Slowly but surely the island was hypnotising her. Never had she felt so completely relaxed and refreshed.

Because of the mysticism of the place, the four hours just flew by. And when she arrived at the estate agents', the assistant seemed to know why she had come. With no preliminaries she immediately stated, 'Once an agreement is signed there is no going back. Sorry, but the flat is yours.'

However, Sally raised her hand before saying, 'I don't think you understand, but I...'

The lady smiled before interrupting with, 'But I do understand; it is you who does not.'

'No. Listen to me. I wish you to take the one-bedroom flat back.' The agent was about to emphasise that she would not when Sally quickly added, 'And exchange it for a two-bedroomed flat, which will suit the needs of my family better.' She squirmed when she thought of how difficult the meeting was going to be with the Bank of Scotland manager in Leith Walk. He was a man you could do business with. But, as he once pointed out to Josie, when she had twice overdrawn her account, he liked to help people provided they stuck to the one mandatory rule, which was that customers must bank their money with the bank and not the other way about!

6

The family, especially Sally, Luke and Josie, felt that they'd had so much to get their heads around in the last few weeks that the last thing they wanted was for them all to meet up on Luke's weekend off. However, they'd promised John Thomson that they would congregate at the Four Marys at three o'clock on the Saturday so they could hear his father Jock's tales about Peggy Mack, their mother and grandmother.

A bonus in this gathering was they would all assemble to say a fond farewell to Angela, who was going back to America.

In the few short weeks she had been in Scotland, she had wormed her way into everybody's heart. Once the initial reason she'd come to visit had been dealt with she had been accepted as family and everybody rallied around her.

She, on the other hand, had more than returned the friendship and loyalty she received, and she especially attached herself to Sally. There was no use in pretending that there were no problems. Of course there were – especially trying to establish a reasonable relationship between Josie and Angela. No matter how hard Sally tried, there was always an undercurrent of reticence and suspicion when she got them together. Sally readily accepted it would take great effort on Angela's part to forgive Josie. After all, had Sally ever understood or condoned her own mother's behaviour? No. *Because*, she thought, *there are some things that are beyond the comprehension of a child.*

On the appointed Saturday afternoon on the stroke of three o'clock, the customers were politely ushered out of the Four Marys lounge. Rita then began to bring in the platters of food for the private party.

John Thomson and his father, Jock, had arrived about two o'clock, and it was obvious that the old man had gone to great lengths to appear respectable for the occasion by donning a dress shirt and his best suit.

Since everyone had assembled for Jock's storytelling session, Sally placed him at the centre of the middle table. She had just got him seated when it became evident that he was over-anxious and to relieve the pressure he was continually drumming his fingers on the wooden table. He was so clearly uptight that Sally wondered, *Why?*

Sally had to put her concern about Jock

aside and get things underway, because at four o'clock sharp a taxi would be calling to take Angela to Waverley Station for the start of her journey home. This being the case, Sally decided she should spend some time with her before she got caught up in her hostess duties.

Taking Angela aside, Sally whispered confidentially, 'Do you have enough money? It would be no problem for me to give you a little something as a sinking fund.'

Angela laughed. It was a light laugh that was so distinctively her. 'Aunt Sally,' she emphasised through her cackles, 'I already have a rescue package that I got from my grandmother, and thanks to you taking me under your wing I have never needed to dip into it.'

'I'm going to miss you. The house will seem so quiet without you bawling out "I'm going home to San Francisco" every morning in the bathroom.'

Angela threw her arms around Sally. 'And I'll miss you. The best thing that has happened to me on this trip is I found out I had an Aunt Sally.'

'And your mother,' Sally quickly interjected.

Angela went on as if Sally had not responded. 'Aunt Sally,' she intimately continued, 'if I send you an invitation to my wedding next year, would you come?'

'An invitation for only me?'

'Well, no. I'll send it for you and a partner and you can bring anyone you like with you.'

'So you won't be specifically asking your mother?'

Angela shook her head.

'Well, in that case save yourself the postage, because I will come to your wedding as your mother's partner, but please understand that Josie is my sister – she had one bloody awful life as a child. I have always looked out for her and I could never be party to anybody hurting or humiliating her.'

'In that case, all I can say is that I love you Auntie Sally and I respect your decision – but remember it is your decision.'

Tears of regret and frustration welled up in Sally, and before she could join Jock at his table, she had to go to the toilet to freshen up.

Emerging from the lavatory, she noticed that Jock was in deep conversation with Daisy, who had also brought along the dashing Dr Falconer. The doctor, to Sally's surprise, was so casually dressed that he looked like a college dropout.

Mincing her way over to the table, Sally, who wished to have her thoughts diverted from Josie and Angela and the problems with their rocky relationship, was pleased to greet Jock. 'Now,' she began with a coquettish smile and a few friendly pats of his hand, 'you, sir, promised me some wonderful tales about my mother and my childhood days, so how about getting started old-timer?'

The undivided attention Sally had poured on him seemed to boost old Jock's confidence, but before he replied, he wiped his whiskers dry with a very, for him, clean handkerchief. 'Just saying,' he began with a long sniff, 'to your sister Daisy here that whenever I look and listen to you and Josie I see and hear your mother.'

'You do?' exclaimed Sally, who didn't wish to be identified with any of Peggy's attributes.

'I do. You see, my dear, you have your mother's energy and drive, but Josie has her stunning looks.'

Daisy and Sally were both rocking with laughter. 'Think that's a backhanded compliment, Sally,' Daisy spluttered.

'Could be you're right,' Sally quipped, while reaching over and gently tugging Jock's beard.

'And, Jock, do you see nothing of my mother in me?'

'To be truthful, Daisy, hen – I haven't given you much thought. It's Peter...'

Sally had been going to twitter again, but the mention of her brother Peter put an end to any further hilarity.

'Peter,' she cried, 'are you saying you knew

my brother Peter?'

Jock was now visibly upset. 'Knew him? Oh, lassie, there's never a day goes by that I dinnae think about him. Regret what happened to him. Like my own faither, he was. Strong, yet gentle. Always trying to please and putting others' welfare before his own.'

'Like your father. What do you mean?'

Lifting Sally's hand in his, Jock began to stroke it gently before saying in a hushed voice, 'Did your mammy never tell you about her and me?'

Sally shook her head. She then tried to take her hand from Jock's, but his grip was so tight she couldn't. She knew she would have to reply to him, but she was experiencing mixed emotions. It was true that she was desperate to learn the exact nature of the relationship between Peggy and Jock, but on the other hand she felt that if it was another sordid episode of her mother's life then she could do without knowing. 'And what about my mother and you?' she whispered cautiously and quietly.

Jock, still fiercely holding on to Sally's hand, began, 'I was just a young strapping man when I met Peggy. I thought as I'd been happily married to my childhood sweetheart for six months and she was pregnant with our first, and only, child that I wouldn't be attracted to any other woman.' He sobbed and cried before going on. 'But the moment

I met your mother I was doomed and so was she. Love-struck with each other we were. Honestly, I wanted to, but I couldn't stay away from her – keep my hands off her. Oh Sally, she was so beautiful and vivacious but she was like hypnotic alcohol – you know you shouldn't drink it because it will destroy you, but you can't stop swallowing it. Then she told me she was pregnant and she wanted me to divorce my wife...'

Mouth agape, Sally wrenched her hand free. 'Just a minute,' she yelped. 'Are you saying that *you* were my brother Peter's father?'

Jock nodded. 'Aye, and to my shame I never recognised him, so he was labelled bastard. You see, I couldnae divorce my wife. I'm staunch Catholic and I'd have been damned forevermore if I'd dared to break my vows.'

'But if it was my mother that you loved then shouldn't you have at least acknowledged Peter?'

'I was going to, but I thought it best to tell my wife first that he was mine. She went berserk. Broke a plate over my heid, kicked me where she shouldn't have and then threatened to kill herself if I mentioned to anyone that I had put your mother in the family way.'

'So your wife knew you had fathered another child but she wouldn't let you tell anyone?'

'Not exactly. She got me to confess it to

the priest down at St Mary's Star of the Sea and he said my duty was to my wife and John. And he suggested that Peggy should put her child in an orphanage.'

'Then what happened?' Sally asked, as the magnitude of the situation her mother had found herself in dawned upon her.

'I stayed with my wife.'

'You never had any more children with your wife?'

'No. You see, you have to sleep together for that to happen and I was sentenced to sleep in the big armchair until she died last year, then I was allowed back in the big bed.'

'And you and my mother never met up after that?'

Jock looked perplexed. 'We did. As you know, I was in the police and unfortunately on the Junction Street beat so I was always bumping into Peggy. If she had Peter with her she would say, "Come on, son, I don't want you mixing with that big, bad man." The wee soul was terrified of me. And I wanted to give your mum a wee something to help with your brother's upkeep, but I had to hand over my wage packet unopened every week. I wasn't even given money for my fags, my Willie Woodbines; she bought them for me. I'd made a mistake...'

'Just a minute,' Sally gasped, 'don't you dare say my brother Peter was a mistake! The only mistake I can see was my mother

getting in tow with you! Don't you understand that I loved my brother? He was good
to me.' Sally grasped the edge of the table as
she tried to keep control. 'Don't know how
I would have survived my childhood without him.'

'I know that. But she goaded me with
him.' Jock was now looking disgustingly at
his right hand and thumping it off the table.
'And see this hand of mine, I wish I could
cut it off for what she made me do to him.'

'What are you talking about? What did she
make you do?'

'He got into trouble. Nothing serious ... he
just stole a couple of pies when you and he
were hungry. Because I wouldn't do right by
your mum, she decided to get even with me,
and any man that fancied her she took. She'd
gone off to Glasgow with her latest lover and
left the two of you. And then when the judge
said Peter would need to go to the Industrial
School for correction, she said no – birch
him.'

Sally knew that she didn't wish to hear the
rest of this story. Somehow she was already
aware of what had happened.

Shaking with the raw emotion that had
been conjured up by his memories Jock continued through racking sobs. 'By now she was
twisted. She knew that I was the duty officer
that day so it would be me that would have to
beat my own defenceless laddie. Smirking

291

she was when she handed him over to me. "When you're done with him," she whispered gleefully, "tell him to make his own way home. I've better things to do than hang around here." With that she flounced out of the station without a backward glance. And see when I was tying his hands and feet...'

Luke, concerned about the state Jock had got himself into, came over to the table and signalled for Daisy to vacate her chair so he could sit down. 'What in the name of heaven is going on here?' he exclaimed, while casting a hostile look towards Sally.

'Just listen,' was Sally's tearful response.

Jock was now completely oblivious to anyone being present except himself, and the desire to confess what he had done to the son, he was not man enough to recognise, was overwhelming him. Stuttering and whimpering through heartbreaking sobs he went on. 'I asked him if I was hurting him. He said, "Naw, mister, I ken you have to dae it." And when I lifted up the birch and landed the first stroke on his back and he screamed out in agony I knew that I was a wimp of a man. I should have stood up to the women in my life, but I never could. And my poor laddie, Peter, bore the brunt of my failures. See when the beating was over, I flung that blasted birch into the corner of the room and I refused ever again to lay a hand on any other laddie. Sponged Peter's back I did, then

292

I sent him home to his loving mother.'

Sally head was now bent so low her forehead was nearly on the table. Luke put his arm around her and he whispered, 'Well, Sally, at least you know who Peter's father was. Isn't that something you have always wanted to know?'

'Oh dear God, please help me to understand. Luke,' she screamed, 'as God doesn't seem to know perhaps you can tell me why my mother and this apology for a man thought they had the right to blight the life of my poor dear brother?'

Luke shook his head. His emotions were in turmoil too. Always he had blamed Sally for not being tolerant of his mother. He had even suspected that she had hastened her end. But had she? 'Sally,' he asked gently, 'was it because of what our mother did to Peter that you suffocated her?'

Sally pushed herself away from Luke. 'I never quickened her end and I'm glad I didn't. Any suffering she was enduring would never, ever have been enough compensation for the cruelty and indifference she dished out.' Sally was now in full flow. 'I admit I jumped up on her bed and I had a pillow in my hand and I was going to smother her. Do you know her dying words were not for you or me, Luke, but for Peter? She wanted him to know she was sorry. Why do people think they can run roughshod over you and then

293

when you can no longer cope with their cruelty, desertion and inhumanity, all they have to say is "sorry" and that will make it alright? "Sorry" doesn't rectify anything and it never will. As to what happened next? Well, didn't poor, misjudged Paddy Doyle realise I was so overwrought that I might do something stupid, so he grabbed my legs. I toppled over, the pillow flew from my grasp, and suddenly Paddy and I were wrestling on the floor. When we got up the pillow was over Mum's face and she was dying. In hindsight, I think she may have pulled the pillow over her own face. Because of that there were no pressure marks and the doctor was more than happy to sign her death certificate. So it's thanks to your dad that I have a clear conscience.'

'His dad?' old Jock mumbled. 'Naw. Naw. You see, Peter wasn't my only child by your mother!' A deep groan escaped him, but it was quickly replaced by a sly smile when his treasured memories floated to the surface. 'You have to understand,' he pleaded, 'Peggy and I were so infatuated with each other that whenever we had the chance we were like two dogs in heat.' He hesitated before adding, 'So after Peter there was you, Sally.'

'Me?' Sally blurted.

'Her?' Luke shouted.

'Aye, and know something else she was always telling me? It was how you wanted to know who your father was. See, when I would meet you in the street I was tempted to tell you.' He hesitated. 'But I knew if I did my wife would find out, and life was already hard enough.'

Sally emotions were running riot. Here was a man she thought was a dear old gentleman, but now he was confessing to being a phil-anderer, a lecher who had fathered Peter and herself. And was he going to add Luke to his stable? Somehow she feared that he was.

She didn't have long to wait because John had now joined them. 'Has he told you the entire shameful story? And me, his legal son as he is always saying, I always wanted brothers and sisters, and I didn't know I had any until my mother died. I knew my parents' marriage was made in hell and they hated each other and I thought they'd probably stayed together for my sake. Och...' He gently laid a comforting hand on Jock's shoulder. 'I just have to accept my dad...' he smiled before correcting himself, '...*our* dad was a randy, irresponsible scoundrel.'

'That right? And exactly how many of his bairns are running about Leith then?' a bewildered Luke asked.

'Just you lot.'

'Are you including me in that lot?'

John nodded. 'Yes, Luke, I am, because as far as I know he was responsible for fathering Peter, you Sally, Josie and yourself. Look, I know it's difficult for you to accept, but you all came about because of a lifelong torrid affair between two irresponsible people.'

Luke was speechless. Sally's mouth gaped. Josie, who had been standing in the background, was trying to swallow her fists, and all was quiet until the bar door was flung open and a voice called, 'Taxi for Angela Yorkston.'

'That's me,' Angela shouted as she grabbed for her coat and picked up her suitcase. 'Aunt Sally,' she said, patting Sally's shoulder to get her attention. 'It's time for me to leave.'

Sally breathed in deeply before rising to take Angela into a strong embrace. 'I'll miss you. Now keep in touch. Angela,' Sally faltered, 'did you hear what Jock was saying?'

Before she responded, Angela took a long breath. 'I did. And...'

'Did it help you to understand why your mother reacted in the way she did when you were born?'

Angela bit her lip before saying, 'I suppose it did. But I still need time.'

Josie had now crossed over the room and she tried to put her arms about Angela, but Angela managed to stave her off. 'Look, darling,' Josie pleaded, 'I'm sorry – truly sorry.'

Angela nodded and she held out her hand to Josie. 'M-m-m-um,' she said, stuttering over the word, 'I don't know if you heard what Aunt Sally just said, but she was pointing out that in some cases "sorry" is not enough. But what I will say to you is that just now, "sorry" is definitely not sufficient to make up for you abandoning me, but given time it may be what we will have to settle for.'

Tears of rejection oozed from Josie eyes, but Angela didn't see them, as she had already turned and was making her way to the door.

It was as if some magic voice had called out to the assembly to rush and say farewell to Angela, because everybody dashed for the door. Unfortunately, Sally, and more importantly Josie, were at the back and could not push themselves forward.

'Oh Sally,' Josie cried. 'She's gone and I don't know if I'll ever see her again. All I wish is for her to look on me as her loving mother, but will that ever happen?'

Enclosing Josie in a strong embrace, Sally whispered in her ear, 'I can tell you, and don't ask me how I know, that you and I will throw confetti over her next year, and in the following years you will become the most travelled member of our family when you are forever jaunting over the Atlantic to see your grandchildren.'

'You really think so, Sally?'

'I know so. And now let's try and make some sense of old Jock's confessions.'

'What do you mean, Sally? He's told you.

He fathered all of us except Daisy. Mind you, you must hand it to Mum for having the audacity to palm Luke off on Paddy Doyle.'

Sally laughed. 'Now, should we not have known? After all, Paddy is short in stature and Luke resembles a long drink of water!'

'Know something? For the first time I feel sorry for Mum. Imagine spending your life being used like an old shoe by the only man you ever truly loved. No wonder she became the she-devil she was.'

'Yeah, and Josie, I also feel so very sorry for Luke. How on earth will he ever be able to tell Paddy the truth – and if he doesn't, will he be able to go on as if nothing is amiss?'

'Talking of Luke, here he comes, and as I am the manageress of this pub, I must go and gather up the glasses.'

Luke sat down on a chair opposite Sally. 'Been some day, has it not?'

'Aye, it sure has.'

'Sally,' Luke stammered, 'I won't be able to sleep easy if you don't ... forgive me.'

'For smashing my face and then attempting to kill me?' she replied, looking him straight in the eye.

'You somehow knew it was me?'

'Yes, and why?'

'Firstly I wouldn't have killed you, because up until today I thought you weren't worth doing time for. Please try...' he reached forward and covered her hand with his, '...and understand that I've always been plagued by thinking of Mum's last minutes and up till tonight I thought you had somehow ... surely I don't need to spell it out. Oh Sally, I only wanted you to have a sample of how frightening it must have been for her if you had.'

'You know, Luke, you have a nerve to ask me to forgive you ... but I do. And why, you're wondering? Well, because sometimes when I'm driven too far I'm afraid too of what I'm capable of. So let's forget the past. We have a future – a good future. So let's call a truce and get on with our lives.'

'Suppose you're right, Sally. And I promise I'll no longer be jealous of you.'

'You – are jealous of me?' Sally exclaimed while pulling her hand free.

'Aye, I have always wanted to be like you, and I'm delighted I'm your full brother.'

Rising, Sally went over to Luke and she put her arms around his neck. 'Know what?' she chuckled as she nuzzled her nose into his cheek. 'The best thing about today is that you, my dear brother Luke, my dear departed brother Peter, my sister Josie and myself have had the good fortune to discover we are all *full* brothers and sisters, because you see...' She now walked over to pat the old tearful man on the shoulder. 'We are all Jock Thomson's bairns.'

Standing up, Luke lifted up his glass of

whisky, and huskily he announced to family and assembled friends, 'Everybody please drink to that!'

The publishers hope that this book has given you enjoyable reading. Large Print Books are especially designed to be as easy to see and hold as possible. If you wish a complete list of our books please ask at your local library or write directly to:

Magna Large Print Books
Magna House, Long Preston,
Skipton, North Yorkshire.
BD23 4ND

This Large Print Book, for people
who cannot read normal print,
is published under the auspices of

THE ULVERSCROFT FOUNDATION

... we hope you have enjoyed this book.
Please think for a moment about those
who have worse eyesight than you ...
and are unable to even read or enjoy
Large Print without great difficulty.

You can help them by sending a
donation, large or small, to:

**The Ulverscroft Foundation,
1, The Green, Bradgate Road,
Anstey, Leicestershire, LE7 7FU,
England.**
or request a copy of our brochure for
more details.

The Foundation will use all donations
to assist those people who are visually
impaired and need special attention
with medical research, diagnosis
and treatment.

Thank you very much for your help.